SWEET DREAMS

Jack Dillon Dublin Tale 2

Second Edition

SWEET DREAMS

Jack Dillon Dublin Tale 2
Second Edition

Mike Faricy

Library of Congress Control Number: 2023920356
paperback ISBN: 978-1-962080-63-7
e-Book ISBN: 978-1-962080-64-4

MJF Publishing books may be purchased for education, Business, or promotional use. For information on bulk purchases,
please contact the author directly at mikefaricyauthor@gmail.com

Published by

MJF Publishing
https://www.mikefaricybooks.com

Acknowledgments

I would like to thank the following people for their help & support: Special thanks to Nick, Roy, Julie, Mittie, and Toui for their hard work, cheerful patience and positive feedback. I would like to thank family and friends for their encouragement and unqualified support. Special thanks to Maggie, Jed, Schatz, Pat, Av, Emily and Pat, for not rolling their eyes, at least when I was there. Most of all, to my wife, Teresa, whose belief, support and inspiration has, from day one, never waned.

"Funny how I keep forgetting you're insane."

- Colleen O'Brien

PRELUDE

S he walked past the building on the corner as she had every day since she first received the news. She fought the urge to pass through the wrought iron gate and enter the office. She wondered what it would be like inside, after all, she'd never been in a morgue. Of course, that led to the next question, did she possess the courage to see her brother? Would she have to see his wounds? Did he suffer?

She did what she always did, lingered on the corner for a minute or two, said a quick prayer in Russian, and hurried back down Griffith Avenue, hoping no one had taken note. She was convinced once she identified her brother, it would only be a matter of minutes before she was deported.

Her brother was gone, murdered by an American, and she knew that nothing she could do would change that fact. But that didn't mean she couldn't repay in kind. She had a sense that it would happen. If there was a God, he would see fit to give her the opportunity. She said another prayer now like she had every day since she first received the news. "Lord God, I pray, I beg only to serve you, let me cleanse the world of this creature, this murderer."

Once she finished her prayer, she picked up her pace and hurried home. She took solace in the fact that if there was a God, a just God, he would surely grant her request.

ONE

After being shot in a Dublin airport attack, US Marshal Jack Dillon was on indefinite loan to Ireland's police force, An Garda Síochána. Only one person appeared to be happier than August Dahlquist, Dillon's former boss, and that was Dillon's attractive hospital nurse, Lin.

"I don't believe it," she said, pushing Dillon's wheelchair into the elevator, not quite able to wipe the smile off her face. They were returning from the meeting in the conference room where the deal had been agreed, transferring Dillon to Dublin.

"Yeah, it's all kind of shocking. One minute I'm getting ready to board a plane, and a little more than seventy-two hours later, Inspector McCabe is lining up a place for me to live in Dublin. Go figure."

"You'll have to give me your new address," she said, then reached down and squeezed Dillon's hand. "I'm sure you're going to need some special attention once you're released from here."

Her insinuation went completely over his head. "God, I wonder where they'll have me stay. Maybe the top floor of some skyscraper, you know, a penthouse forty floors up. Or maybe some fancy country estate they confiscated from a crooked banker. Maybe—"

"No offense, Marshal, but as far as confiscating property from crooked bankers, well, we have plenty of them, but none of them have been charged, let alone prosecuted. And the tallest building in Dublin is supposed to be the Exo building, that's only going to be seventeen stories, and it hasn't been built yet. Just a thought here, I've always got a guest room that's just going to waste. Or...."

"Seventeen stories? That won't work. Guess it'll be the country estate," Dillon said as the doors on the elevator opened, and Lin pushed him out into the hall. For the briefest of moments, she thought she might just wheel him over to the geriatric wing and leave him parked in the hallway. How could one person be so dense?

"Maybe one of those fancy places on the south side? I'm sure they, hey, careful, God, Lin, for a moment there, I thought you were going to run into that tray of bedpans. Not the best way to end the day," he laughed.

Lin just bit her lower lip and decided she'd have to up her game. She pushed the wheelchair down the hall and back into Dillon's room. "Here we are, back in the same day," she said, then set the brake on the chair so Dillon could climb out.

"Thanks, Lin. I appreciate all the help you've given me. I wish there was some way I could repay you."

She raised an eyebrow and said, "Well—"

"You run a really tight ship here. No offense, but I've never been a fan of hospitals, and to be honest, the last time I actually had to stay in one I'd just been born," he said, then laughed at his own joke.

"Thank you. I just wondered, I hope you don't think I'm too forward," she said as he climbed back into the hospital bed. "Were you seeing anyone back in the States? I mean, are they going to fly your girlfriend over or something?"

"Seeing someone? Good God, no. I didn't—" There was a knock on the door, and then someone pushed it open.

"Oh, I'll check in on you later," Lin said when she saw who was standing in the doorway and then hurried out of the room, pushing the wheelchair.

TWO

Inspector McCabe and a rough-looking guy stepped into Dillon's hospital room. McCabe looked frustrated.

"Bit of bad news I'm afraid, Dildo," McCabe said.

Not for the first time, Dillon promised himself if and when he ever got back to the States, he was going to kill whichever of his pals had passed on his nickname.

"Thought we had a place lined up, but the current tenant seems to be taking her sweet time leaving. I have it on good authority…" He glanced at his thuggish looking accomplice for a moment. "I have it on good authority that she'll be vacating by tomorrow. In the meantime, you can continue to enjoy your posh surroundings," he said, then held his hands out to encompass the hospital room.

So much for a comfortable surrounding. There was a bank of monitors just behind Dillon's bed, although he was no longer hooked up to them, and they were all turned off. Still, lots of equipment and cords not needed at the moment. Mercifully, the bed next to him was empty and would remain so. As far as anything to interject some sort of personality into the room, there was a crucifix hanging on the light grey wall next to the door, and a television mounted up close to the ceiling near the bathroom. The prestressed concrete ceiling had a seam running down the center. If you were in bed, the window had a pleasant view of the sky, today cloudy and threatening rain, but if you stood next to the window and looked down a floor, you got an unobstructed view of the dumpsters, two blue and one green.

"Here, a little light reading material to keep you busy tonight," McCabe said, setting a six-inch file on the table tray. He pulled the table away from the wall and rolled it in front of Dillon. "Just some general information on our order of battle, who does what to whom. You're on the back page, and I'd be remiss if I didn't remind you that shit flows downhill."

"Gee, thanks," Dillon said, glanced at the six-inch file in front of him, then diverted his attention to the grey sky out the window.

"Oh, cheer up," McCabe said. "Things are bound to get worse. Give it to him, Pat, before he tries to sneak back to the States. I'll see the likes of you, tomorrow," McCabe said, then turned on his heel and headed for the door.

The rough-looking guy reached down toward the floor and brought up a brown paper bag. The bag appeared to be holding a bottle. He waited until McCabe was out of the room before he pulled out a bottle of Paddy's Irish whiskey.

"Wanted to make sure he was out of the room before you saw this, he's not supposed to know. Pat O'Malley, by the way. Pleased to meet you."

Dillon extended his hand, and O'Malley shook it. "Thanks. You didn't have to do this." He nodded at the bottle.

"You'll need something to help you get through that file. All right then, I'll leave you to it and hopefully see you tomorrow. Oh, and don't let them catch you with that bottle. It's against the rules," O'Malley chuckled.

"Nice to meet you and, ahh, thanks," Dillon said, then watched him as he left the room. He took the bottle, examined the label for a minute, then shoved the bottle down under his blanket. He opened the file, took a deep breath, and started reading.

THREE

H e'd worked his way through a good two-thirds of the file, remembered a handful of names, but had forgotten most of the others. It wasn't as bad as it looked since government policy required all documents had to be in both English and Irish, so half of the six-inch file was an unreadable repetition. At a little after eight, he heard a subtle knock on the door.

"Hey, how we doing? Still awake, I see."

Dillon looked up to see nurse Lin walking in, only now she wasn't dressed in blue hospital scrubs.

"Hey, Lin, how's it going? Wow, look at you, hot date?"

She was dressed in a short, tight, dark blue skirt. Very short and very tight, with a "V" neck cleavage that barely contained her. She smiled as she approached and held a small silver purse on a chain in her right hand. As she slowly strutted toward him, she spun the purse in a circle. Her steps looked practiced as if she was slowly strutting down a fashion runway, and he noticed the stiletto heels matching her dress. She strutted, placing one foot directly in front of the other, accentuating her hips, bouncing that wonderful chest with each and every step.

"Just wanted to check in on you, see how you were doing. I heard the good news. Guess we're hanging onto you for another day. Thought I'd maybe stop in, gaze at our good fortune and make sure you were okay." She raised her eyebrows as she came alongside his bed. "Mmm-mmm, I'll give you this, you look…great."

"Thanks, Lin. I have to tell you. Things are starting to look decidedly better now that I've seen that dress. Jesus."

"What? This old thing?" she said, then bent down, apparently looking at the hem that had just risen up another inch, exposing a good portion of her backside. Right now, Dillon would have killed for a mirror on the far wall. As she leaned down, her full breasts seemed to fight in an effort to escape the confines of her dress, and for half a moment, Dillon wondered if he just reached out, could he—

She straightened up, flashed a sexy smile, and set her purse down by the foot of the bed. She grabbed the hem of her dress with both hands, lifted it up for a half-second, exposing a nanosecond of red thong, and gave a slight tug, bringing it back down over her backside. "Maybe scooch over a little. I don't want to sit in that plastic chair. It'll be too cold."

He couldn't blame her. The orange plastic chair was a molded thing that looked like a remnant of whatever passed for modern fifty years ago. He began to slide over, then remembered the bottle of Paddy's whiskey under the covers. Not sure exactly what to do, he placed his right arm down over the blanket, at the same time raising his right leg, and then in one quick motion, he slid the bottle over and between his legs as he moved sideways a few inches.

Lin climbed up onto the bed, exposing another quick flash of her red silk thong in the process, then snuggled up next to him. "Mmm-mmm, not too bad. Kind of comfy," she said, moving her hands around and perhaps inadvertently patting his upper thigh a few times. "God, if you can believe it, I've never been in one of the hospital beds before. Honest, I'm not fooling."

"You gotta be kidding me," Dillon said.

"No, really. I mean, we always joke about sleeping in an empty room, but, well, first of all, there are never any empty rooms, and then, to be honest, we never have time to sleep. There's always something to be done."

"What about the night shift?"

"God, you sound like one of the accountants. If it was up to them, they'd make the maintenance staff redundant, and then we could mop floors and clean rooms while everyone slept. Of course, they forget about medications and emergencies. I mean it is a hospital after all. So, anyway, first time in a hospital bed, and gee, and it's with you. Just you and me, alone in bed, Jack," she said, then gave a little shrug and just stared at Dillon for a long moment.

"Yeah, think of the possibilities, all the traction devices, and the different ways the bed can raise up."

Lin's eyes flared. She swallowed, then gasped, "God, the possibilities, you're telling me." She rubbed his thigh up and down a few times, then slowly moved her hand up to about his navel before she made a slow, but very direct beeline down between his legs.

Dillon closed his eyes as her hand slowly traveled across his navel, then continued on its journey south. "Mmm-mmm," he moaned, then waited.

Lin's eyes widened, she felt her face flush and realized she was suddenly panting in time to the movement of her hand. She closed her eyes and let a soft moan slip out from between her lips.

Dillon was still waiting for something to happen. He could feel her gently rocking alongside him, heard her moaning. He opened one eye, glanced down, and saw that she had her left hand wrapped around the neck of the whiskey bottle resting between his legs. Her right hand had slipped beneath the hem of her skirt, and she let another soft moan escape from between her lips. Eventually, her movement began to dwindle in intensity, and once she appeared to be finished, he gently removed her hand from the neck of the bottle and kissed it.

It took her a long moment to recover. Her chest stopped heaving, her face returned to its normal color, and he could hear her slowly begin to return to a more normal breathing pattern. She blinked a few times before she flared her eyes and said, "My God, man of steel. You Americans. If I could lock this door from the inside, I would." She slid off the bed, exposing her gorgeous rear in the process, then tugged the hem of her short dress again.

"Wow. I'm, like, oh wow!"

Dillon shrugged like it was just an everyday occurrence.

She reached for her purse at the end of the bed, opened it, and pulled out a business card. "Here, this has my address and phone number. Be sure to call. I promise it'll be worth your while. I'm on second shift tomorrow. Hope you're still here," she said, then turned and walked away. She stopped at the door, looked back at Dillon, and said, "Amazing!" just before she hurried out the door.

Dillon reached down between his legs, pulled out the bottle of Paddy's and stared at it for a long moment, thinking, *You're getting more action than me.*

He went back to reading through the file, pausing every ninety seconds or so to replay Lin's all-too-short visit. Then he studied the card with her address and phone number. He would have given her a call, suggested she make a return visit, or maybe he could just grab a taxi and head over to her place, but there wasn't a phone in the room. He'd ground through another page in the file, replayed her visit, then read her card again. He wondered if they'd maybe let him borrow the phone at the nurse's desk for a few minutes, then read another page in the file, beginning the process all over again. Eventually, he drifted off to sleep.

FOUR

McCabe spun the wheelchair alongside the hospital bed. "Hospital policy, we've got to wheel you out." Dillon lay on the bed, dressed in a pair of ill-fitting trousers and a shirt with the sleeve cut off. His left arm was safely bundled in a sling, although he felt his healing had progressed to the point where he didn't need the thing.

"I just told you, I can walk. I've got a shoulder wound, for God's sake. My legs and feet are just fine."

"Sorry, hospital policy," O'Malley growled. "We always follow the rules. Besides, look at it from their point of view. Something happens to the likes of you, and they'll have to put up with you for another day or two. After all they've done, that certainly wouldn't be very fair," he said, then slapped a massive hand against the back of the wheelchair.

"Yeah, well as long as you put it that way," Dillon said and settled into the wheelchair. He placed a white plastic bag stuffed with his few possessions on his lap, then gave the nod for O'Malley to proceed.

"You do the honors, Pat," McCabe said and headed out the door.

O'Malley waited a moment then half-whispered, "You got that bottle of Paddy's, right?"

"What? Oh, no, gee, sorry about that," Dillon said. "Bit of a party last night, and then finished the rest for breakfast."

"You finished it? Oh, would you ever just feck off," O'Malley laughed, then just for revenge took off at a fast pace, avoiding the door frame by a quarter of an inch at the very last minute.

"Jesus, would you watch where you're going, man? You're gonna have me back in the ER before I even get out of this place," Dillon said, which only brought a laugh from O'Malley, and he headed down the hall even faster.

"Say goodbye to the lovely ladies," McCabe said as three nurses in blue scrubs stood behind the nurse's station and waved. Dillon recognized two of them, smiled, then held up the card he'd gotten from Lin last night, and nodded.

She pursed her lips as if giving a kiss and winked at him. O'Malley whooshed him past. The nurses all laughed and waved as Dillon headed down the hall.

Lin called after them, "See you later."

The car was parked right outside the door in a no-parking zone, a white SUV sort of thing with blue letters on the doors and across the front of the hood that read "GARDA." A set of flashing lights was mounted on the roof.

"Pat, you grab the back seat, Dildo, you hop in the front passenger seat. You need a hand?"

"I think I can make it," Dillon said and climbed in, quietly groaning to himself. He buckled up, and a moment later, they were on their way, lights flashing.

"I think you're going to like the place we've lined up for you," McCabe said. Dillon caught him looking at O'Malley in the rearview mirror. He slowed to a stop at the corner, quickly checked traffic left and right, then just drove through the red light.

"A, umm, *'friend'* to the service was staying there up until recently…"

"Last night," O'Malley interjected.

"…so it's pretty much furnished, bed, linen, towels, cooking utensils. Enough there that you can get whatever else you need at your leisure. You have the rest of the week off. You'll begin working in earnest next Monday. But not to worry, I've brought along a stack of files you can review in the interim to bring you up to date on how we attempt to function in general, and some specifics of the operation you're going to be on."

"You're basically going to use me as bait for the Russian mob?"

O'Malley laughed from the backseat.

"That sounds a bit harsh," McCabe said as he glanced over. "Let's just say we can use your expertise, and by the same token, it's likely that bunch of wankers will take an interest in you."

"Do they know I'm out of the hospital?"

"As far as we know, they think you're already back in the States. I'd like to keep it that way until we're positioned. You go through those files, I think it will help you get a better handle on things."

"What about communication?"

"Communication?" McCabe said.

"Yeah, is there a phone? What if I need help or a doctor, or I don't know, maybe directions to your office?"

"We'll handle all that tomorrow. We've got to get you an ID, an office pass, the usual mumbo-jumbo of paperwork. Make a note, Pat, he'll need a vehicle, too."

Dillon marveled at the foot traffic as they hurried through the streets. Sidewalks teemed with people of all ages. Bicycles moved with the flow of traffic on opposite sides of the street. They crossed over the Liffey on the Samuel Beckett Bridge and took a left on the far side.

"Lucky you," McCabe said. "We've got you on the south side of the city, Dublin Two. It's a trendy, posh district, just like you, Dildo."

"All us real Dubs live on the north side. It's mostly bankers and thieves in Dub 2 and 4," O'Malley said from the back seat.

"Then I should fit in just fine," Dillon said, which earned him a laugh and a pat on the shoulder from O'Malley. They followed the Liffey for a couple of blocks, then slowed before taking a right and waited for a senior citizen to cross the street.

"Bleeding, eejit plonker, and we've got the flashers on and everything," O'Malley groaned.

"That's your new home up there on the left. You're on Townsend Street," McCabe said.

All Dillon could see was a building painted purple, with a massive sign hanging across the front that read "The Windjammer," and below that, "Open at 7 AM".

Dillon looked across the street at the Windjammer and said, "You've got me staying in a pub?"

McCabe made a quick left turn at the corner and pulled into a no-parking zone. "What? No, a pub? For God's sake, Dildo, over here, this building," he said, and pointed to the brick apartment building he'd just parked in front of. The building looked to be four stories tall, with white trim and a series of small porches hanging out over the sidewalk marking a number of the units.

"Looks like nice digs," Dillon said, tilting his head to see the top of the building. He opened the door, groaned as he carefully climbed out of the car and onto the sidewalk, then took another look at the building.

"Come on inside, and you can examine your estate. I think you'll like it," McCabe said and hurried out of the car. O'Malley went around to the back of the car, and pulled out a paper shopping bag striped pink and white, and what looked like Dillon's suitcase from the back of the car.

"You grabbed my luggage from the Gresham?"

"What?" McCabe said and glanced back at O'Malley. "Oh, yeah, of course. Room charges through Saturday night went to your former employer, the Marshals Service. I'm sure they'll only be too happy to accommodate. The Gresham gave you a pass on the next five days since you weren't actually there, and, well, they're bound to get some good press that won't be costing a bleeding cent. Promised them we'd mention it in all our news briefings," he laughed.

McCabe punched a four-digit code into the security lock, and the metal front door clicked open. "Here we go, home sweet home," he said, then stepped inside. O'Malley held the door for Dillon, then followed them in with the suitcase and bag.

They walked down a short hallway, neatly trimmed and painted an off-white color. Their footsteps echoed across the polished granite floor. They turned left, and McCabe pressed the button for the elevator. Classical music seeped out from behind one of the apartment doors as Dillon walked past. The elevator opened a moment later. McCabe gave Dillon a wink and said, "Please, Dildo, after you."

FIVE

It was a slow rickety ride up to the third floor before the elevator stopped. They waited for what seemed like an awfully long pause before the doors finally opened. "Just to the right at the far end of the hall," McCabe said, and then the two of them followed Dillon off the elevator and down the hall. The floor was deadly quiet, and for a brief moment, Dillon wondered if anyone else even lived up there.

The last unit was 328. McCabe took out a set of keys that were attached to a bright pink wristband, unlocked the door, then handed the wristband with the keys to Dillon.

Dillon looked at the wristband, a bright florescent pink, with white letters that spelled out "Sinéad."

"Nice and bright, so you don't lose them," McCabe said.

"Who's Sinéad?" Dillon asked.

"The former tenant. Nice girl. Unfortunately, she decided to move in a hurry," McCabe said, and then followed up with a disingenuous smile. "What say we have a look," he said and pushed the door open.

There was a short hallway that went off to the right and a bedroom immediately in front of them. The bedroom door stood partially open, and Dillon caught a glimpse of a bed. He walked down the hall, past a bathroom on the right-hand side, and into a small living room. A black leather couch, an end table with a lamp, and a cabinet with a small flatscreen TV opposite the couch stood at the far end of the room. A glass-topped coffee table sat in front of the couch. A door centered on the far wall led outside to a small porch with a view of the Windjammer pub, in all its purple glory sitting directly across the street. The porch had a white metal railing around it and appeared to be just large enough to accommodate two people, provided they both remained standing.

The kitchen was immediately behind them, at the opposite end of the room from the porch and the Windjammer. It looked to be almost, but not quite, as large as the closet in Dillon's bedroom back in New York.

Among its limited features were no more than two feet of countertop space, a two-burner stove, a refrigerator small enough to fit under a desk, and a sink just barely large enough to accommodate a dinner plate. The room was illuminated by a bare lightbulb positioned in the center of the ceiling. A string hung from the light to turn it on and off. What looked like a food and water dish for a dog sat on the floor in the corner of the kitchen.

"A dog comes with this place?" Dillon asked, indicating the food and water dish with a nod of his chin.

McCabe looked to O'Malley for an answer.

"Not a worry, it's all taken care of. The little fellow's off keeping some lonely, broken-hearted woman company and won't be back." Then he walked toward the far end of the living room, set the pink and white striped bag on the coffee table, and nodded at the bag. "More files, for your reading enjoyment," he said and laughed. "Should be enough to keep you out of trouble."

McCabe appeared anxious to leave and said, "I guess we'll let you get settled in here. We'll maybe pay a visit tomorrow morning, make sure you're okay. You need anything, there's a Eurospar just down the lane. Questions?"

"No, I think I'll be okay."

"All right then, I guess we're off," he said, and the two of them headed for the door. McCabe stopped at the door and called back into the living room, "Oh, and keep a low profile now, nothing too crazy." Then they both laughed, closed the door behind them, and were gone.

Dillon watched out the window and waited. They were still laughing as they stepped out of the front door, climbed into the SUV, and drove off. He remained in sort of a state of shock, not sure what to think. Once the SUV disappeared around the corner, the place seemed suddenly quiet, too quiet for Dillon's taste. He picked up the remote, clicked on the small flatscreen to get some noise in the room, then began to look around and take in his new surroundings.

He opened the small refrigerator and found two bottles of white wine, one of which was half-empty. The freezer held one ice cube tray, minus maybe half of the ice cubes. One shelf in the kitchen cabinet had three dinner plates, two bowls, and two mugs. The shelf above held a half-dozen assorted glasses, each sporting a beer logo; Heineken, Budweiser, Carlsburg, Smithwicks, and two Guinness glasses, all no doubt pinched from a local pub.

The bathroom featured a half-roll of toilet paper, an almost empty tube of toothpaste, and a container of woman's moisturizing body wash. Three bras and three thongs hung from the shower curtain. Dillon felt the inclination to check the bra size, a thirty-six C-cup.

He walked down the short hall and pushed the bedroom door open. The bed was made and looked to be a double size as opposed to a queen or king. Thankfully, it was made, although he could see what looked like a head imprint on the pillow.

A small closet stood at the foot of the bed with a white metal bifold door. As he opened the door, it squeaked loudly, and then he just stood and stared. The closet was full of clothes on hangers. A woman's clothes. Just the slightest scent of perfume, not necessarily unpleasant, drifted out into the room. Pairs of high heels, tennis shoes, and boots littered the closet floor. He opened the top drawer on the dresser positioned next to the bedroom door. Socks, lots of socks, along with more thongs and bras. It seemed that whoever had been here either left in a hurry or they expected to return shortly.

He grabbed his suitcase from the living room, wheeled it into the bedroom, and unzipped it. He placed his clothes on top of the dresser; three pairs of boxers, three pairs of socks, two t-shirts, all in need of a wash. He made a mental note to himself. He'd have to find a washing machine in the morning and, right after that, a clothes store to expand his wardrobe. He took the unopened bottle of Paddy's whiskey, Lin's favorite, and placed it in the cabinet beneath the small flatscreen in the living room.

He poured himself a glass of wine from the opened bottle on the refrigerator, then settled onto the couch, pulled the stack of files from the pink and white shopping bag, and began reading.

The wine was sour, not that he really cared. In short order his thoughts were directed toward Lin and the card with her phone number. About a second after that, he recalled that she was going to be working second shift, which meant she wouldn't be off until ten. Not that it really mattered all that much, because his next thought was that he didn't have a phone.

He returned to the files, took a sip of the sour wine, got up, poured the remainder of the glass down the sink, then did the same with the remnants in the bottle. He decided to leave the other bottle unopened and returned to the couch and the stack of files. He jerked awake sometime after eleven, turned out the lights in the living room, checked the lock on the front door, then padded into the bedroom, and went to sleep.

SIX

He woke early the following morning. Without really moving, he could roll partway over and lift the cheap white Venetian blinds covering the bedroom window. The sky bore a grey cast, not from clouds, but rather from the early hour. Dillon stared for a long moment, then watched as a bus drove up the side street, rolled past the Windjammer, and out of sight.

He thought it was nice to know he was on a bus route, although it had been years since he'd taken one. Still—

He guessed the time at maybe six in the morning, then checked his watch and found out he was off by an hour, and it was just a little after five. He lay in bed for another fifteen minutes, then finally got up and walked to the bathroom. Once finished, he wandered into the kitchen and searched the pantry cabinet for, God forbid, coffee and something to eat. There were a couple of cans of dog food which didn't necessarily appeal to him, two cans of tomato soup, a can of mushroom soup, a jar of pasta sauce, but unfortunately no pasta. He did find a coffeemaker in the far back of the cabinet and could only hope it worked.

He showered using the woman's moisturizing body wash while staring at the bras and thongs still hanging from the shower curtain. He made a mental note to pick up a razor and shaving cream along with some food necessities, then dried off with the towel hanging from the hook in the bathroom.

He dressed, and even though his shoulder was stiff, he decided not to wear the sling. He found a pencil tucked between the two cushions on the couch and an empty envelope in a recycling bag beneath the kitchen sink. He sat down and began to write a grocery list, listing coffee as the first item. When he had finished, he had maybe twenty items penciled in on the list. He folded it, slipped the envelope into his back pocket, grabbed the keys attached to the fluorescent pink wristband, and headed out the door.

He wasn't sure where, exactly, he was headed except that the Eurospar was his destination. At this hour, there was no one on the street to ask for directions, so he headed off toward the bright lights three blocks away. He eventually found the Eurospar only to learn he was twenty minutes early since the shop didn't open until 6:30. He waited on the sidewalk until the store opened.

He was joined by a short, red-faced guy in desperate need of a shave, a clean set of clothes, and most likely a shower. The guy was having trouble standing and attempted to stagger around in a large circle. Eventually, he took a seat on the low concrete wall alongside the shop. About two minutes before the shop opened, he passed out and fell backward into a garden so that just his feet remained up on the wall. His right shoe, actually a well-worn work boot, had a large hole in the sole.

Dillon walked over just to check on him. He looked down over the wall to where the guy was lying on his back. There wasn't any blood, at least that he could see, and it looked like he'd just fallen back no more than a foot and a half, landing in a bed of mulch. He was still breathing, snoring actually, so Dillon left him there, then went back to the sidewalk in front of the door and entered into the shop once it opened.

He picked up a red plastic basket with handles from a stack next to the front door, then worked his way through his shopping list as he wandered around the store. He added a couple of important items, KitKat bars, a bag of Snickers, a box of ice cream bars, and a bag of caramels then headed toward the checkout lane.

There were only two people in line ahead of him. The first was a woman purchasing a box of teabags who was dressed looking like she was heading to work. Behind her yawned a sleepy-eyed guy purchasing a package of Pampers and some baby wipes. He looked like he'd been rousted out of bed. Dillon paid for his purchases, bagged them himself, and headed back to the apartment.

He set the two grocery bags on the kitchen counter, filled the coffee maker with water, added the grounds, set the maker on the stovetop, and plugged it in. Then he said a prayer until he heard what sounded like water beginning to flow over the coffee grounds. He pulled one of the two mugs out of the cabinet, set it on top of the stove, and proceeded to unpack his purchases and put them away.

Once the coffee was made, he poured a cup, took a long sip, and declared it the best cup he'd had since he had arrived in Dublin. He carried the cup with him out into the living room and set it on the coffee table next to the stack of files. His shoulder began to throb, and he slipped his sling back on. He glanced at his watch and then out the window, almost 7:30, and traffic was beginning to pick up. The occasional person now walked past the Windjammer, presumably on their way to work.

He opened the next file in the stack and started to read. The file covered the kidnapping and murder of Oisin Kelly, a thirty-two-year-old male, originally from the town of Arvagh, in County Cavan, population nine-hundred-twenty-five.

It seemed Mr. Kelly, a known Dublin drug enforcer, was killed when his car veered off a straight stretch of highway on a clear summer's day and into an oncoming semi. Along with Mr. Kelly, his wife, Aidine, age twenty-nine, daughter Niamh, age three, truck driver Russell O'Leary age forty-seven and his passenger, Timothy Walsh age twenty-three, were also killed.

Investigators determined Kelly's vehicle experienced an explosion from a planted device set off by a timer. Not that the folks who planted it cared about collateral damage. The report went on to state that Kelly had made contact with members of the Russian mob while vacationing in Spain's Costa del Sol. He'd organized a major drug purchase, and then apparently refused to pay—a bad business decision.

Dillon read until midmorning, working his way through close to a dozen more case files similar to the Kelly file in a number of ways. The Russian mob was either strongly suspect or, as in two instances, arrests of Russian individuals had actually been made. In all but two instances, a drug enterprise was directly involved in the murder. In the two instances where drugs were not directly involved, a protection racket with a tangential relationship to a drug territory played a part, along with, again, either a lack or refusal to pay.

Dillon was interrupted by a knock on the door around eleven. He cautiously made his way to the apartment door, peeked out, saw McCabe, and behind him, O'Malley.

"Gentlemen," Dillon said as he opened the door.

"How goes the battle, Dildo?" McCabe said, stepping in and heading for the front room.

"Depressing," Dillon said, following the two of them. "I've been reading about all these nice Irish guys who end up blown to bits in exploding cars, or in one case tied to railroad tracks. I thought that that went out with Snidely Whiplash." Dillon laughed.

Both McCabe and O'Malley turned and stared at him with a blank look.

"Oh, sorry, an American cartoon from when I was a kid. Guess you didn't get it over here."

"We're battling the fecking Russian mob, Pat, and your man is fantasizing about cartoons he watched as a bleeding child. Jaysus."

"Makes for interesting reading, doesn't it," O'Malley said. "Gives you an idea what we're up against. Car bombs seem to be one of the preferred choices, but they're not beyond just beating some poor bastard to death. Who was the one they staked out in the snow over in Scotland?"

"MacManus," said McCabe. "Beat the shite out of the miserable bastard, then stripped him, literally staked him out on the ground in a snowstorm, and left him there."

"Pissed on the bastard before he died. I don't think they found him until spring, course, by then it was a little too late," O'Malley laughed.

"Nice bunch of lads," McCabe said, then reached into the paper bag he was carrying and pulled out a small box. "Here you go, this will do for the immediate future. You're good to go with ten euros on it." He handed the box to Dillon, containing a small pay-as-you-go cellphone. "You can top it up at any Centra store, they're all over Dublin. We'll get you lined up with something a little more heavy-duty, but this should keep you connected for the next week or so. You got the numbers?" he asked O'Malley.

O'Malley pulled a wrinkled piece of paper out of his front pocket and handed it to Dillon. Dillon glanced at it.

O'Malley's, McCabe's, and a general office number were written down.

"Thanks. Hopefully, I won't have to call you."

"No one hopes that more than us," McCabe said. "All right then, we'll leave you to it. Let you get on with your studies, as it were. We'll stop by tomorrow morning, bring you into the office, give you a chance to meet and greet folks. You got anything else, Paddy?"

O'Malley shook his head.

"Then we're off. Remember, keep a low profile. I'd like certain people to think you're already out of the country. Till tomorrow then. Enjoy," McCabe said, giving a nod to the stack of files before they headed out the door.

SEVEN

illon ate a quick lunch of smoked salmon with a couple of slices of brown bread, then returned to his stack of files. He hadn't been reading all that long, maybe just a little over an hour, when there was a soft knock on the door. He thought about ignoring it, then decided maybe that wasn't the best idea, so he quietly walked to the door. Whoever it was knocked again, this time a bit more forcefully, just as he was about to peer through the peephole. He looked out and saw the top of a woman's head, dark hair, parted down the middle. She took a step back and casually glanced down the hall. She wore glasses, was not unattractive, and appeared to be alone. He thought for a moment, then cautiously opened the door.

"Good God, you've your thumb up your hole or what?" she said, then looked up at Dillon and grew wide-eyed. "Oh, sorry. Umm, can I speak with Sinéad?" she said, and sort of looked past Dillon in an expectant manner.

"Sinéad?" he said. "I think you've got the wrong apartment."

"The wrong apartment?" She stared at him, then focused on the sling holding his left arm. "No, this is Sinéad's place. I was just here the other night. Where is she?"

"I don't know. I only arrived yesterday afternoon. I'm living here," he said, hoping to end the conversation.

"You American?"

"Yes, and you are?"

"Sinéad's friend. We, umm, sort of *work* together, *freelance,* you might say." She looked past him again, this time trying to peek into the living room.

Oh Christ, he thought. Then, before he could stop himself, he said, "Would you like to come in? My name is Jack, by the way, Jack Dillon. I'm not sure I caught your name," he said and held out his hand.

"I didn't give it," she said, ignoring his hand. She quickly stepped past him and hurried toward the living room. She sort of stood in the middle of the room and slowly turned around, looking like she expected to see something and was suddenly disappointed. "Where in the hell is she?"

"You got me. I've never met the woman."

"What about Lucifer?"

"Lucifer?"

"Never mind. When did she leave?"

"No idea, but I'd say she took off in a hurry. She left behind a closet full of clothes, the dresser in the bedroom is still full of lingerie. A bunch of shoes are in the closet."

"Oh?" She suddenly sounded interested and hurried past him into the bedroom. He heard the closet bifold door squeak as she pulled it open. By the time he looked into the bedroom she was on her hands and knees, pulling shoes out of the closet. There were far more pairs than he had originally thought. She seemed to be in the process of sorting shoes into two separate piles. She tossed stiletto heels, fancy sandals and the like on one side, and workout shoes on the other.

"I'm going to have to get rid of all these outfits. Do you know somewhere I can take them? I'm pretty new to Dublin."

"You don't want them?" she asked, still sorting through shoes. At the moment, she was holding up a pair of red stilettos with sparkling silver heels and toes.

"Me? No, not really my style, besides I don't think they'll fit."

She glanced up, then flashed a smile. "I suppose I could maybe have a look, see if there isn't something that might work."

"Tell you what, all or nothing. You can have whatever you want, but you have to take it all. Oh, and you have to tell me your name."

"Sorry about that, thought you were maybe just an overnight *guest*. I'm Abbey. Pleased to meet you," she said and extended her hand.

He reached down and shook it. She responded with a firm grip and a nice smile. Her term '*guest*' wasn't lost on him.

"What happened to your arm?" She nodded at the sling.

"Oh, work-related accident, my shoulder actually. Nothing special. I'm in the recovery mode now. You know how it goes, it always seems to take a little bit longer than you expected."

"Yeah. Wow, there's lots of stuff here," she said, sitting back on her heels and taking in the piles of shoes, two pairs of boots, and all the outfits on hangers crammed into the closet.

"Yeah, and don't forget that chest of drawers." He stepped over and pulled two of the drawers open. The top drawer was filled with socks and undergarments. The next drawer contained all lingerie, lots of lingerie. More than a few of the items had sequins on them.

Abbey rose up off her knees, stepped over to the dresser and began to quickly rifle through the drawers.

"God, she must have left in an awful hurry." She seemed to think for a minute, glanced again at the outfits crammed into the closet, then pulled out a phone. "You mind if I call a girlfriend? She's right here in the building, just the floor below, and about the right size."

"No. If she can help get all this stuff out of here it would be just fine with me. Give her a call."

She was already dialing, and a moment later spoke into her cellphone. "Hi, you in? What? I don't know anything about that. Here, come-'mere to me now, I'm up in Sinéad's. No, the stupid slapper's gone, taken off. Umm, there's a guy who moved in. Want's to get all of

Sinéad's stuff out of here. No, free just for the taking, anything you want, but we have to take everything. Yeah, in fact, I'm looking at both pairs right now," she said, glancing at the two pairs of knee-high leather boots leaning against the wall. "Yeah, come on up, and we can start hauling all this shite over to my place. Okay, yeah, bye, bye, bye," she said and hung up.

"Okay, she's on her way up. She'll be here in a couple of minutes. We'll cart all this over to my place. I'm just down the hall from you. Once it's in my flat, we can take our time sorting through everything."

"Gee, I wish I could help you, Abbey, but doctor's orders, you know, no heavy lifting," Dillon lied, then glanced at his sling for added emphasis and flashed a sort of pained expression.

"We'll get it."

"There are a couple of things hanging in the bathroom, too. Not sure if they fit, but you can have them anyway," he said, trying to make used underwear sound like the bargain of the century.

There was a knock on the door a moment later. "There she is," Abbey said, and hurried past him. She opened the door and squealed, "This is our lucky day. Come on and meet our new neighbor." She stepped back into the bedroom a second later.

The woman following behind her had sandy brown hair, brown eyes that sparkled, and a wreath of flowers tattooed around either wrist. She was wearing blue jeans, skin-tight blue jeans that showed off attractive thighs and a firm behind. She wore a faded, green t-shirt emblazoned with the white letters, "U-2". She appeared to have an average breast size, and Dillon figured she wouldn't be interested in any of the bras.

Abbey sort of bounced up and down a few times like an excited school girl and said, "Jack Dillon, meet my friend Gemma. She's the biggest slapper in the building," she said.

"Slapper?"

"American?" Gemma asked, and looked to Abbey.

"It means slut," Abbey said.

"I'm only the biggest slapper when you're not around," she said to Abbey. "Nice to meet you, Jack is it?"

"Yeah, Jack Dillon." They nodded at one another but didn't shake hands.

Gemma eyed the closet crammed with clothes, got a puzzled look on her face, and asked, "Where did Sinéad go?"

"I've no idea," Dillon said. "I only just arrived the other night. To tell you the truth, I was more than a little surprised to find all this still here. But obviously, I'm not going to be wearing any of it. I was halfway thinking of donating it to some sort of charity, but if you girls can use it, well, that would seem to be a far better option. Like I said to Abbey, help yourself, but you have to take all or nothing."

"Not like her to leave all this," Gemma said, looking just as puzzled as Abbey had a few minutes earlier. She eyed the two pairs of knee-high boots leaning against the wall and hurried over. She picked up the black pair with the gold toecaps and set them against the wall. "Okay with you?" she asked Abbey.

"Yeah, plenty of time for all that later. We'll cart all this down the hall to my flat, and we can sort through it in private. Guess we may as well get started," Abbey said, then stepped over to the closet, grabbed an armload of clothes and wrestled the hangers off the closet rod. "Go ahead and grab a pile, Mrs., and we'll bring them down to my place," she said, then headed for the door.

"Here, let me get that," Dillon said, then stepped out of the bedroom and opened the apartment door. Gemma wrapped her arms around a number of items, then sort of groaned as she wrestled them off the closet rod, a handful of hangers bounced onto the floor, and she followed Abbey out the door.

Dillon wedged the heel of a pink shoe under the apartment door so that it remained open. He stepped back into the bedroom and began taking clothes out of the closet and placing them on the bed. He had the closet pretty well empty by the time the two women returned.

There seemed to be a number of very nice outfits that still had the price tags attached. Even on hangers, they looked sexy, and he thought their friend Sinéad must be a woman with some rather expensive tastes.

Once they returned from their second trip, he took a chance and said, "I really appreciate this help, ladies. I don't have anything here to cook, but if you'd pick a place, I would gladly buy you dinner tonight once you've finished."

They looked at one another, and Gemma nodded.

"Okay, yeah, we can do that," Abbey said. "Maybe give us a bit of time to get cleaned up once we haul all this out of here."

"And you're sure she's gone, Sinéad?" Gemma asked as she gathered up another armload.

"Yeah, I'd say she just up and left, based on everything still hanging in the closet and all the clothes in the dresser."

"Funny she wouldn't say goodbye," Gemma said, sort of shaking her head.

"Something about a gift horse comes to mind," Abbey said as she began emptying the top dresser drawer, piling the items on top of the dresser. "Gemma, go see if she doesn't have some shopping bags tucked back alongside the fridge. We can use them to get all this in just one or two trips."

Gemma hurried out of the room and was back a moment later with a stack of shopping bags with handles, a few of the usual brown paper grocery bags, but then a bright pink bag, a yellow one and a couple of white ones with some sort of fancy logo on the front.

Dillon removed himself to the living room and started reading files again. He'd been seated on the couch for a good half-hour when he heard the women giggling out in the hallway. A moment later they both stepped into the living room.

"That's all of it, Jack," Abbey said and gave him a smile.

"Can't thank you enough, ladies. You still interested in dinner?"

They both nodded eagerly, then Abbey said, "Give us an hour to get cleaned up, and how 'bout we meet you at the Ginger Man?"

"The Ginger Man?"

"It's just up on Fenian Street. Walk up that way, and you can't miss it." She pointed up past the Windjammer. "Take a left, and it's on the corner. We'll see you there. Sound like a plan?"

"It does. I'll see you there in an hour."

"Make it an hour and a half," Gemma said.

EIGHT

They'd finished their meals. Dillon managed to get absolutely no information from either woman as to what they did for a living. But, then again, he was the one who told them he had a boring government job. He had ordered another round and then one more round after that. They were lingering over the last of their drinks when the couple who'd had their picture taken with Dillon outside approached the table. The woman who'd left the lipstick on his cheek gave him a friendly wave.

"Would you mind letting my friends have their picture taken with you?" she said and nodded toward two other women standing just behind her. Both women smiled and nodded excitedly.

Abbey and Gemma suddenly stared at one another with surprised looks on their faces. Before Dillon could say anything, all four people had crowded around him.

The woman who'd left the lipstick smear pushed three separate cellphones across the table toward Abbey as everyone huddled around Dillon. He received kisses from the two ladies, and then the woman who'd left the red lipstick smudge earlier kissed him again, this time leaving a smudge on the opposite cheek. They departed, saying thanks over and over again, then stopped and chatted with the barman on their way out the door.

"You have got to be kidding me. What in the hell was that all about?" Abbey asked, wide-eyed.

"Any lipstick smudges? I just hate it when that happens. Turns off all the other women who want to kiss me," Dillon joked.

"Oh shut up, and here," she said, then leaned over and began dabbing at both sides of his face with her napkin. "Really, Jack, what was that nonsense all about?"

He looked at both women for a long moment, decided he'd better come clean. "It was because I was involved in that shooting, the one that happened last Sunday out at the airport."

"Explain 'involved.'"

"I was one of the people they tried to kill."

"Oh my God," Abbey suddenly screeched. "You're him, aren't you? You're the American." She indicated his sling with a nod of her chin. "You're the one who shot them."

"And then they shot you," Gemma said.

He moved his right hand, hoping to indicate they could maybe keep their voices down. A few heads at some of the tables around them were looking over in their direction. Two women at the table next to them leaned together conspiratorially and started talking in an animated conversation.

"Oh. My. God. Why didn't you say something? You call that a work-related injury? For God's sake, you were shot, you fecking plonker. It was even on RTE and in all the newspapers."

"Could you just keep it down a little? We…"

Abbey was up and handing her phone to Gemma. She stepped alongside Dillon, and he put his arm out so he could wrap it around her waist.

"Piss off. There'll be none of that. Just push your chair back," she said as more heads turned toward their table.

Once he moved his arm, she suddenly stepped between his legs, quickly sat down on his lap, and struck a sort of XXX pose that had her almost bursting out of the top of her dress. She took his head in both her hands, shoved it into her cleavage, and planted a massive kiss on the center of his forehead. All the while, Gemma kept taking pictures until Dillon was almost blinded from the flash.

He waved her off. "Okay, okay, that's enough. Come on now, you're making a scene. Stop it, please." Abbey stood up, tugged at the hem of her short skirt, then stepped to the side so Gemma could take her place, and the routine started all over again. Except that, Gemma, once seated on Dillon's lap, began to move in a way that could only be described as a lap dance. And she didn't stop.

Eventually, both women settled back into their chairs. Just as they finished their drinks, the barman suddenly appeared, carrying a tray with another round of drinks along with three shots of whiskey.

"Proud to have you here, mate. I wonder if you wouldn't mind joining me at the bar for a quick picture. It'll only take a moment. I've got your man over there waiting." He turned and glanced at the bar. Dillon looked in the same direction. A guy in a suit coat and a t-shirt with a camera around his neck gave a sort of half-hearted wave in their general direction and smiled.

"A picture?" the barman said again, then sort of indicated the tray of drinks he'd just brought over. At least he didn't want to sit on Dillon's lap. They ended up taking a good half-dozen photos at the bar before Dillon was able to make his way back to the table. Two more rounds of drinks were waiting, and four more couples were hoping to have their picture taken. It went on like that for the better part of the rest of the evening.

Dillon thought they'd only been there for an hour or two when suddenly the lights came on in the place, and a few minutes later, the entire pub broke into a song called the "The Parting Glass." Dillon could only remember the chorus, "Good night and joy be with you all."

Amazingly, Dillon, Abbey, and Gemma were able to pour ourselves into a taxi and make it home.

The pounding on the door woke Dillon the following morning.

NINE

The pounding wouldn't stop, or was it just in Dillon's head? He struggled to pull on his boxers, then turned at the sound coming from the other side of the bed. He glanced over, squinted, and detected a female figure lying up against the wall with the pillow pulled over her head.

The pounding started up again, this time louder and even more forceful. He quickly closed the bedroom door, took a deep breath in an effort to steady himself, then stumbled to the door and looked out the peephole.

McCabe and O'Malley. A frustrated-looking McCabe shook his head and pounded again just as Dillon was looking out the peephole. Dillon's head bounced off the door. "Dildo, you fecking knacker, open the damn door. Dildo!" McCabe called, raising his voice.

"Hey, Dildo," O'Malley yelled even louder.

Dillon opened the door, stood in front of the two of them in just his boxers with one hell of a hangover.

"Oh, well, thank you for finally answering the door. Good morning, your highness. I hope we're not too late," McCabe said. He stared at Dillon's boxer shorts for a long moment before barging past and heading into the living room.

"Here, nice job of following directions on your part. Wonderful," O'Malley said and thrust a newspaper and a large cup of Starbucks coffee at Dillon, then followed McCabe.

Dillon followed behind. McCabe was staring out the porch door, apparently studying the purple paint on the Windjammer pub just across the street. He turned to face Dillon, who had just shuffled into the room, still trying to clear his head.

"It appears you lost no time making yourself comfortable," he said, staring down at the coffee table. An empty bottle of Paddy's whiskey and three glasses were scattered across the table.

Dillon noticed a pair of red high heels resting under the couch, most likely belonging to whoever was still asleep in the bedroom. He didn't think McCabe could see them from the angle he was at, at least he hoped so.

McCabe picked up one of the glasses and held it toward the sunlight, examining the lipstick along the edge. "Seen the paper yet this morning? Go ahead, be my guest."

Dillon set the Starbucks cup down on the end table and opened up the newspaper. There was a picture of him on the front page, just below the fold. The image took up roughly a quarter of the page. In it, Dillon was standing next to the bald, overweight barman from last night. Their arms were draped over one another's shoulders.

"Nice, and it's not even my best side," Dillon tried to joke.

"Does the term 'low profile' even mean anything to you?"

"Hey, look, it's not my fault someone recognized me. One thing seemed to lead to another and well, I mean, the next thing I know, all these hot, gorgeous Irish women wanted their picture taken with me."

"Your barman is anything but hot and gorgeous. So based on your experience, you decided it would be a good idea to get the newspaper involved? On the front page, no less?"

"Must be a slow news day. Look, I didn't know the photographer was with a paper. I had absolutely no idea. The barman just said he wanted a picture with me, and this guy happened to be there with a camera around his neck. How was I supposed to know he was with a newspaper?"

"Oh, for God's sake, go put something on, please. You're in the process of ruining any appetite I might have had for lunch."

O'Malley sort of chuckled and opened the door to the refrigerator as Dillon hurried back to the bedroom. He couldn't recall who it was in bed, Abbey or Gemma? Whoever it was, by the time he hurried back into the bedroom, she'd pulled both pillows over her head.

The woman in the bed had three red roses tattooed on her backside. The design was positioned in such a way as to make it appear that the stems of the roses were being held together by a very gorgeous bum. Dillon stopped for a brief moment and appraised the artwork.

"Dildo, come on, let's get going, we've tons to do, and we haven't got all day," McCabe called from the living room.

Dillon reached across the bed and adjusted the blinds, so whoever was sleeping or passed out wouldn't be disturbed by the sunlight creeping into the room. Then he slipped on the same clothes from last night. He quietly pulled the bedroom door closed and headed into the bathroom. At least the thongs and bras weren't hanging from the shower curtain any longer.

He stepped back into the living room. The pair of red high heels that he'd first spotted under the couch were now neatly arranged on the coffee table, sitting next to the empty Paddy's bottle and glasses. Dillon thought it might be best not to acknowledge them.

"Well, now at least we know how you earned your nickname," McCabe said and headed past him toward the door. O'Malley followed, smiled, and gave him a thumbs-up as he passed. "And don't forget your keys," McCabe called, then headed down the hall toward the elevator. Fortunately, Dillon had left the keys in his pants pocket, and he quietly pulled the door closed behind him.

They had parked on the street in the same no-parking zone as the other day. He noticed they were constantly scanning around the area as they headed to the car. He climbed in the front passenger seat, O'Malley hopped in back, and McCabe settled in behind the wheel.

"First order of business is some lunch," McCabe said, then looked over toward Dillon. "You look like you could use it. Is that?" He leaned closer to Dillon, wrinkled his nose in disgust, and sniffed a few times. "Don't tell me that's Viva La Juicy you're wearing?"

"Viva what?"

"Viva La Juicy. Did you find a jar of that shite in the place? It's the perfume the slap…err, former renter—"

"You mean Sinéad?"

"…used to wear. Yeah,Sinéad. How is it you were able to come by her name? You tell him?" he asked O'Malley in the backseat.

"More importantly, the bigger question is, what happened to her?" Dillon said. "She left all her clothes behind, didn't seem to take anything with her. What happened? Where did she go?"

McCabe turned on the blinker, waited for a car to pass, and calmly made a U-turn. O'Malley gazed nonchalantly out the window and looked like he wasn't paying attention to the conversation.

"What happened to her?" McCabe finally said. "Some not very nice people found out she was working with us. They're pals of your friends from the airport. She was a working girl, and the majority of that industry has fallen to this Russian gang. Once they learned she was helping us out, the bastards put a price on her head, and we thought there just wasn't time to neatly pack things up. We were lucky to get her out of Dublin alive. If you've been reading those files, you'd know they don't seem to take too kindly to people helping us."

"So if I've moved into her unit, hours after she fled the scene, what does that make me? Some kind of target?"

"Well, we didn't think that would be the case, at least initially. It's the main reason we had hoped you'd keep a low profile. Of course, that was before you thought it would be a good idea to get your picture on the front page of the paper. Right now, it seems to be a bit of a roll of the dice to know what the bastards are thinking."

"The good news is none of those bastards can read, so they'll never see the paper," O'Malley laughed from the backseat.

McCabe glanced at him in the rearview mirror. "We'll get you a vehicle, set you up with some funds, a bank account, a tour of the office, such as it is. You've got your cellphone?"

"Yeah, right here," Dillon said and patted his front pocket. "What about issuing me a weapon?"

"We plan to take care of that, too, although need I remind you, things are just a little different over here. We're certainly not the Wild West, and we don't intend on becoming such. "

"Yeah, I get that part, really, I do. Now no offense here, but do you guys have any sort of plan other than trying to nail these jerks when they try to kill me? Reading those files, they seem rather efficient when it comes to that line of work."

"We're working on it," McCabe said, then pulled to the curb in front of a pub and opened his door. "Come on, time for some sustenance. I always think much better on a full stomach."

Over lunch, they told Dillon what they knew about Sinéad, which didn't seem to be all that much.

"She worked for these bastards, they paid her rent, gave her a little, and I mean very little, spending money. Bought her lots of fancy clothes. Took her nice places where she could see and be seen."

"And what? Was she an informant?"

"Not at first. She was just someone a few of the fellows on the force sort of knew. And…"

"Sort of knew? You mean they had some sort of a working relationship with her? What?"

"I suppose you could characterize it like that, a working relationship. Then someone beat her up, one of the bad guys. She didn't say anything. My guess is she thought it came with the job. The third time it happened, she landed in the hospital with a broken jaw. That's when she got in touch with us and said she had something to tell us if we could provide her protection."

"And what did she tell you?"

"Time and place of a robbery. They were going to hit a post office up in Glasnevin. See, the old wans, they do a lot of their business at the post office. They pay bills through their pension accounts, which are usually maintained by the post office."

"Pension accounts? You mean like a bank?"

"Yeah, exactly. Anyway, the post office is loaded with cash on the third of the month, and a bunch of elderly folks are waiting in line to get at it. There's virtually no security at the post office. One of these Russian plonkers, a sometime boyfriend, slaps Sinéad around the night before the robbery and decides to prove how important he is by telling her about the robbery that's going to happen the following day, and then he dumps her. She tells us, we're there waiting for them and nail all four of them. That was, oh, nine, ten months ago. Anyway, somehow they recently found out she was our source. The twat who slapped her around while he bragged was found hanging in his cell on Monday. That's why we had to move fast."

"Any chance these guys are going to come knocking on the door?"

They both scoffed, and O'Malley said, "Probably not, even now that you made the front page. Or at least they won't show up looking for Sinéad. On the other hand, they now know that you're still in town. Maybe they'll be able to put it together and figure you're in the area, but that's a bit of a long shot. Still, they'll be looking for you, that's for sure."

"Which is why we'd better get a move on and get some things lined up for you. Check please," McCabe called to the barman as O'Malley and Dillon headed for the door.

TEN

Dillon was able to open a bank account after some heavy persuading of the bank officer by McCabe. He got a quick tour of their office, which was like any government office anywhere in the world. The place featured an elevator that was out of order, twice as many folks as the office was originally designed for, and a lovely view of the brick wall just eighteen inches outside the window.

After a round of introductions and names Dillon immediately forgot, they drove across town to a shooting range where he had to qualify with a nine-millimeter pistol at a distance of fifteen feet before they could issue him a sidearm. He qualified.

"Wasn't sure if they were going to ask you to fast draw that weapon," O'Malley laughed.

"That's only in the movies."

"So where'd you learn to shoot? That was an awfully tight grouping on your target," McCabe asked. He sounded like he expected something along the lines of Dillon grew up with a cowboy father.

"I'm an American, we all shoot that way."

McCabe scoffed and said, "Come on, we'll get you back to your apartment. We can stop at a Tesco on the way, and you can lay in a few groceries. You can't continue to live off candy bars and coffee."

Dillon ended up with four bags of groceries.

The three of them stepped onto the elevator in Dillon's building. McCabe and O'Malley each carried a grocery bag, Dillon carried two bags, and his wounded shoulder was beginning to throb again from the effort.

"You planning on doing a lot of entertaining?" McCabe asked.

"The cupboards were just about bare, and the few things that were left behind I'm really not too sure about, so I'm tossing just about everything out as soon as I get back up there."

Eventually, the elevator groaned its way to the third floor and the door slowly opened. Once O'Malley stepped off the elevator the thing seemed to jump an inch or two. O'Malley was a big guy, but not that big, and Dillon made a mental note to investigate the location of a staircase.

Thankfully, whoever had ended up in bed with Dillon the night before had left, and the apartment appeared to be empty, although just the faintest scent of perfume seemed to linger in the air.

Dillon and McCabe set their grocery bags on the coffee table, next to where the red stilettos had been. If they noticed that the heels, the glasses, and the empty bottle had been removed from the coffee table, and that the apartment seemed to be, somehow, a bit cleaner, neither one commented. The stack of files at the far end of the coffee table looked to have remained untouched.

"I plan to call you Monday morning before I pick you up. We'll get a vehicle issued to you at that time. Have those files I gave you committed to your memory by then," McCabe said, indicating the stack of files on the coffee table. "I want to hit the ground running."

"Enjoy the weekend," O'Malley laughed. Then he nodded at the pistol holstered on Dillon's belt. "Maybe keep that near, and try not to appear in the newspaper this weekend." Then he followed McCabe out the door.

Dillon double-checked the lock on the door, then waited until he heard the doors close on the elevator. Alone in the apartment, he hurried into the bedroom. The Venetian blinds were up, and the bed was neatly made. He still had no idea if it had been Abbey or Gemma who'd spent the night with him, but then the memory, hazy as it was, sort of flickered in his mind and a picture of the two of them walking into the Ginger Man broke through the haze. Both of them had turned a number of heads, and Dillon suddenly recalled that Gemma had been wearing those boots with the gold toe caps, which meant Abbey had worn the red stilettos, spent the night, and had the roses tattooed on her backside. He knew she lived somewhere on the same floor, but he didn't know which unit. Instead of going down the hall and knocking on every door, he decided to just put the groceries away.

He was in the process of boiling some pasta noodles when there was a loud knock on the door. He quietly hurried to the door, double-checked the weapon holstered on the back of his belt, and looked out through the peephole. He stared at the top of Abbey's head just as she looked up and attempted to look through the peephole. He waited a moment then opened the door.

She looked surprised to see him. "Oh, so you're here. Where'd you go this morning?"

"Some work things I had to take care of. I didn't want to wake you. How's the head?"

"Getting better, I've sort of been in the recovery mode all day. Mmm-mmm, you cooking something?" She sort of sniffed the air, then attempted to look past him toward the kitchen.

"I managed to get to the grocery store and pick up some basics. You feel like staying for dinner?"

"Depends on what you're having."

"What I'm having? I'm serving something you don't have to cook. How does that sound?"

"Perfect."

"It's pasta."

"Let me go get a bottle of red wine. I…"

"You don't have to do that."

"I wasn't going to go out and buy some. I've got one in my kitchen. It's even unopened. Give me just a minute, and I'll be right back," she said, then hurried back down the hall.

"Hey, Abbey," he called after her. "Which unit is yours?"

"Three eighteen," she said over her shoulder. She was heading back to Dillon's apartment, carrying a bottle of wine thirty seconds later. He noticed she returned to his apartment barefoot.

"Oh wow, this is great, and a Chianti too," he said as she handed him the bottle and stepped inside. "Let's hope my jar of pasta sauce lives up to this wine."

"I'm sure it will. You, ahh, always go around like that?" She indicated the pistol holstered in the small of his back with a nod of her chin.

"I'm afraid so, at least for the time being. A bit worried those guys from the airport have friends who aren't very nice. Does it bother you? I can put it away if it makes you uncomfortable."

"Uncomfortable? No, not really, I guess it's just different, that's all. It must be more of an American thing."

They had a passable dinner. Dillon had a glass of wine, and Abbey had a half-glass. The residual effects from the Guinness, not to mention the bottle of whiskey, from the previous night, were probably still affecting them. They chatted about almost everything except Abbey waking up in Dillon's bed.

He learned she was from a small town in County Cork and that she'd come to Dublin at the age of nineteen to find her fame and fortune. Thus far, she'd found neither. She was purposely vague about what she did for a living. "Oh, a little of this, a little of that, just about whatever you like," she'd said.

He just nodded, didn't pursue that last particular phrase and moved on to who lived in the building. She left before nine, telling him she planned on going to bed early.

Dillon casually glanced out the window a little after ten and saw a woman crossing the street. She looked familiar, dressed in heels and a short skirt. Eventually, he recognized Abbey, although he had no way of telling if she was wearing one of the outfits that had belonged to Sinéad.

As she crossed the street, a car parked along the curb flashed its lights a couple of times. She hurried over and climbed in. Presumably she talked for a minute or two with whoever was behind the wheel, then the headlights flashed on, the engine fired up, and the car drove away. Dillon didn't pay much attention and returned to working his way through the stack of files McCabe had left for his weekend entertainment. He went to bed a little after midnight and slept the whole night through.

ELEVEN

At just about the same time, over on the south side of Dublin, a blonde woman paid her taxi fare, then climbed out of the backseat and waited until the taxi disappeared from sight. Once the taillights went around the distant corner, she took a deep breath, smoothed the front of her skirt, then walked through the gate and up the circular drive toward the brick mansion.

It was only the second time she'd been asked to call on Alexei Bazanov. The first time, barely two weeks ago, she'd arrived all excited and in awe only to find out that her younger brother Borya had been killed by an American.

The news stations had mercifully been unable to find her, and over the course of seventy-two hours, they'd lost interest and moved on to another disaster. She had been summoned earlier this afternoon on Alexei's behalf and told to arrive at ten. She glanced at her watch, then picked up the pace a bit so she would ring the doorbell exactly at ten.

She checked her watch after ringing the bell and smiled, just ten seconds after the appointed hour. She nervously brushed her hair away from the sides of her face, rolled her shoulders a few times to get the kinks out, then stood straight and tall, waiting for the door to open.

It was the same man who had answered the door the first time she was here. He was large, very large, with a shaved head and dark, close-set eyes, and a long nose, almost rodent-looking in a way.

"I'm here to see Alexei Bazanov," she blurted out in Russian once the door opened.

"Yes, Miss Fedorov, of course. Won't you come in? Mr. Bazanov has been expecting you. Please, this way," he said and gave her a smarmy sort of smile. He remembered thinking there were a number of unnatural things he would enjoy doing to her for a few hours, before discarding her altogether. That thick blonde hair, her ripe body just begging to be taken, her almost childlike face, innocent-looking, although he was aware she was anything but innocent, yes, he remembered her. Who could forget?

She studied him from behind as she followed the giant along the grand hall in the mansion, beneath the elegant plaster cornices and ceiling, past the two massive mahogany doors and the large oil paintings in their heavy gilt frames hanging from the walls. She remained careful to keep her distance. There was a scent she seemed to pick up, danger, violence, and she felt that she wouldn't truly be safe until she entered Alexei Bazanov's office.

The giant stopped at the office door next to the grand staircase. He looked down at her, licked his lips ever so subtly, then gave an ever-so-slight leer just before he knocked.

He took hold of the elaborate brass doorknob and opened the door. "She's here, Miss Fedorov," he said, then opened the door wider and smiled as she walked past him. He had planted himself in the middle of the door frame, and she had to physically brush against him as she entered the dimly lit room. As she did so, he exhaled, hot, foul breath that blew against her cheek, moved her hair, and caused her to momentarily wrinkle her nose.

"Ahh, Miss Fedorov, thank you so much for coming at this late hour, and on such short notice," Alexei Bazanov said. He was seated on a long leather couch that rested against a far wall. The brass lamp sitting on his desk gave off a dim glow, and the two leaded glass lamps resting on the end tables at either end of the couch barely lit up the area. He stood as she hurried past the giant, and if he noticed the wrinkling of her nose, he didn't let on.

He was dressed in dark trousers, and a starched gold shirt buttoned all the way to the neck. Over the shirt, he wore a loose-fitting silk robe. The robe hung open as he stood, the silk belt hung loosely at his side.

"May I offer you a glass of wine? It's a very nice Medoc, a Château Margaux," he said, picking up the bottle, ready to pour.

"Yes, ahem, that would be very nice, thank you," she said, although she had no idea what would be a good wine.

"Please, have a seat," he said once he'd filled her glass. He indicated the couch with his hand, then appraised her as she demurely took a seat. They clinked glasses, and each took a small sip. He seemed to study her for a long moment, running his eyes over her figure.

"So, tell me, how are you doing?"

"Just fine, thank you."

"You've adjusted to your brother's untimely," he paused for a long moment, "passing."

She took a healthy sip, two gulps just to help. "No, actually, I don't think I'll ever adjust. There will always be an empty space there, a large empty space." She took another swallow of wine, this one a bit more subtle. "To be honest, I'm not sure I would want it any other way. He was my younger brother. The baby of the family. I feel responsible in a strange way."

Bazanov nodded like this made sense, and in a way it did, or at least it suited his purposes for the evening. He reached behind him, pulled out a newspaper, and placed it on her lap.

She gave a questioning look.

"The photo there in the lower-left corner, the man, not the fat, bald one, but the cocky fellow next to him, smiling, laughing and no doubt drinking up a storm last night. Do you recognize him?"

She glanced at the image, studied it for a second or two, then looked up at Bazanov and shook her head. "No, I'm sorry, but I don't. I've no idea who he is."

Bazanov nodded, took a small sip of wine, and said, "That's the man who killed your brother."

Her eyes widened. She set her glass on the coffee table, picked up the paper with both hands, and studied the image. After a very long moment, she set the paper down and said, "I told you I would kill him. I still want to."

He smiled and gently shook his head. "You did tell me that, but that's not going to happen."

"But he killed my brother," she said, not meaning to raise her voice, then tried to swallow the lump that was suddenly in her throat. "He deserves to die. You can't let him live. Please, let me—"

He raised his hand, calmly, politely, quieting her. "I agree with all you say. Until that picture, we were led to believe he had hurried back to the United States. Now that we know he's still here, we'll find out where he is, and he will be eliminated."

"Can I—"

"No." He shook his head gently. "I only wanted to let you know I haven't forgotten. We'll find this man, this Jack Dillon, and bring justice to your brother, avenge him. You have my word."

TWELVE

Dillon was up at the crack of eight the following morning, made coffee, then breakfast, and started in on McCabe's stack of files again. The mob, largely Russian and a few Lithuanians, seemed to be rather busy killing Irish drug lords in Spain, running protection rackets, selling drugs, controlling prostitution, and setting up legitimate business fronts for all their criminal activity. He read through the noon hour, and at about two in the afternoon, he started to nod off. It was the scratching that eventually woke him.

At first, he tried to ignore the sound and go back to sleep, but it seemed to grow more persistent with each passing moment. He kept his eyes closed and tried to do a mental map of where, exactly, the noise was coming from. Finally, the scratching stopped, and then, just about the time he dismissed it as a figment of his imagination and began to drift back to sleep, it started up again, only now much more aggressively.

He slowly climbed off the couch and gradually followed the sound toward the door. He cautiously peered out of the peephole but failed to see anything, although the sound was definitely coming from the other side of the door. He gently placed his hand against the door, felt the vibration, and visualized some thug down on his knees, working to pick the lock.

He pulled his pistol, stepped back from the door, quickly turned the knob, and yanked the door open. Instead of some muscle-bound thug working the lock, a small black dog with a leash tied to the doorknob hurried into the apartment. He stopped for a moment, looked at Dillon, bared his teeth and growled. There was a note attached to the doorknob by a green bandaid with red stars. The feminine-looking handwriting read, *"Sorry, but I can't deal with Lucifer any more. P.S. This bad boy is aptly named."*

He presumed whoever wrote the note had tied him to the doorknob and then disappeared back down the hall. Since this was a secure building, the individual who returned him probably lived in the building. All of which did nothing to help the immediate situation.

Lucifer gave a long growl at Dillon again, then barked. Dillon cautiously unwrapped the leash from the doorknob. Lucifer growled once more before making a beeline for the bedroom. He jumped up onto the bed, circled once or twice before he settled down, and stared at Dillon with evil brown eyes. Dillon decided to clean up the pile of dog shit out in the hall in front of his door before he dealt with the dog.

He filled the food bowl on the living room floor from a can of dog food that had been left behind. He filled the water dish, then returned to the couch and the files he was reading. Lucifer made an appearance about forty-five minutes later and gave Dillon a disdainful look on his way to the dog food. Once he'd eaten and had a drink, he gave another disdainful look on the way back to the bedroom.

Around seven that evening Dillon, stacked the files on the coffee table, then walked to the bedroom and said, "Outside?"

At the sound of Dillon's voice, Lucifer's head popped up. He seemed to consider Dillon's offer for a brief moment before he jumped off the bed. He walked over and stood by the door, then looked up. Dillon cautiously grabbed the end of his leash, and together, they headed out the door. They walked the two blocks down to the Liffey, strolled along the river for a bit, then walked two blocks back up to Townsend Street and headed for home.

For the most part, Lucifer was fairly well-behaved, other than barking at some senior citizen walking her dog, a large Alsatian which apparently couldn't be bothered. The woman on the other end of the Alsatian's leash was a little different story. She hurled a string of invectives at Dillon, all the while shaking her head and waving her hands. As a final, parting gesture, she gave Dillon the finger, then rounded a corner and disappeared from sight, all the while continuing to rant.

Back in the apartment, Lucifer actually sat by the door and let Dillon unhook his leash. He hurried up onto the bed, circled twice before settling down, and then gave a throaty growl in the event Dillon had some crazy idea about lying down on the bed that evening. Dillon quickly decided the couch would serve just fine as a comfortable alternative tonight.

He settled in front of the flatscreen, then spent the next hour jumping from channel to channel in the hope of finding something worth watching. He never did. He glanced around the room and discovered a half-dozen books on the bottom shelf of the cabinet holding the flatscreen, five paperback romance novels, and a hard-cover copy of <u>Fifty Shades of Grey</u>. He curled back up on the couch, opened the hardcover, and started reading. He drifted off to sleep three and a half hours later.

THIRTEEN

For Mikhail and Kostya Orlov, it was a dream come true, their big chance to prove themselves to *the* man, Alexei Bazanov. He'd actually contacted them. Just imagine, out of everyone vying for the man's favor, he'd chosen the two them, provided them the opportunity to prove to him just how valuable they could be to the organization.

They'd parked just down the street from the Windjammer pub, and waited in the car for hours, hoping to garner some sign, any sign, that their target was home. They never saw so much as a shadow in all that time.

"Maybe he's not there," Kostya suggested, peering through the car's back window.

"He has to be there, Bazanov said this is where he was living. He must already be asleep," Mikhail replied.

"He could have gone to a pub?"

"Yes, but they closed over an hour ago, and he would be home by now."

"Perhaps he's ventured out of town," Kostya said.

"This is where he's hiding. I tell you, he's up there, probably sleeping."

"Sleeping?" Kostya thought that didn't sound right. "With the lights on? That doesn't seem right."

"This diagram," Mikhail said, not for the first time holding the hand-drawn sheet of paper out for his brother to see. "It shows the layout. The light is on in the living room, the dark window to the right, that's the bedroom. The light has been off since we arrived. I tell you, he's up there, sound asleep. All you have to do is go up there, open the door and fire at the bed until you run out of bullets. There's nowhere for him to hide, and he won't hear you anyway."

"But if he's not there?"

"Enough. Give me the gun. I'm going up there. I'll be the one," Mikhail said, thinking he could be home right now, rolling onto his wife instead of sitting in a cold car with a brother who, after all the tough talk, suddenly seemed to have lost his courage. "Come on, give me the gun. I'm sick and tired of waiting."

"No, I'll go. Besides, you'll never be able to pick the lock. You'll never even get in," Kostya said, suddenly resigned to the task.

"Then go, please. If we don't do this, we'll have a lot more to worry about than picking some cheap lock. Come on, Kostya, go."

"All right, all right, did you hear? I said, I'm going. You'd better hope he's up there."

"I know he's up there, and I know he's asleep, my brother. You remember the code for the front door?"

"4224," Kostya replied.

"And the unit."

Kostya made a face. "At the end of the hall, 328."

"Perfect," said Mikhail. "And that's the hardest part, remembering the code. Now go. I'll wait for you."

Kostya nodded, seemed to think for a long moment, then suddenly gave his brother a quick kiss on the cheek, opened the car door, and hurried across the street.

"God be with you," Mikhail whispered, then watched as a moment later, his brother disappeared into the building.

FOURTEEN

t first, he thought he was dreaming, but the growl, low and guttural, eventually invaded his sleep. It was long and deep, and as he opened his eyes and removed the book resting over his face, he realized Lucifer was standing in the living room doorway. In the dim glow of the lamp, he could just make out the figure of the small, black dog.

Dillon sat up just as Lucifer seemed to retreat a few steps. A moment later, a bright light suddenly illuminated the hall as the apartment door opened. It all seemed to happen in fractions of a second. The door opened, heavy footsteps stomped across the hall into the bedroom, and then the shooting started.

Dillon was off the couch in a second. Lucifer hightailed it across the living room, took a sharp right, and headed into the kitchen, squeezing as best he could between the little refrigerator and the wall. The shooting stopped, and a light flashed on in the smoke-filled bedroom, then someone shouted what sounded like a curse. A figure backed out of the empty bedroom, mumbling, just as Dillon rounded the corner. Using all the strength he could muster, he clobbered the individual over the head with the hardcover copy of <u>Fifty Shades of Grey</u>.

The body crumpled to the floor, then groggily rose to his knees and fumbled with a knife of some sort, slashing out blindly in every direction.

The official version would be that Dillon identified himself as a law enforcement official, told the individual he was armed, and to drop his weapon. When he raised his weapon, Dillon had no way to know the weapon was empty and was left with no choice but to defend himself. That was the official version.

What really happened was, when the guy rose with the knife, Dillon stepped back, pulled the pistol from the holster at the small of his back, and shot him twice in the head. A moment after that, he heard a car screech out on the street. He guessed it was an accomplice pulling away from the curb, but he couldn't know for sure. He dialed 911 a number of times but never got through. It was only later that he learned the Irish Emergency Services number was 999.

But someone did get through to Emergency Services, probably a number of people. Dillon heard sirens just a minute or two after he shot the intruder. He took the intervening time to search him but didn't find anything. He picked up the knife and set it in a kitchen drawer. Four cops were in the hallway a few minutes later. They called in through the open door, and Dillon called back, telling them that it was all clear. He told them he was in the living room, and the body was in the bedroom.

FIFTEEN

Someone obviously contacted McCabe. He arrived about forty minutes later. He apparently had a bit of a reputation, because the five uniforms standing around in the living room with Dillon all gave him a nod, and two addressed him by name, "Inspector McCabe." All of them quickly deferred to him, and then just as quickly left Dillon alone with him in the living room.

McCabe was wearing jeans and a sweatshirt, looking like he'd just pulled them on and hurried out the door in the middle of the night. His eyes still had a bit of a sleepy look, and he needed a shave. He rubbed both hands over his face for a moment, seeming to have left any semblance of charm at home. "What the feck?" he said as the last uniform left the living room.

"That doesn't begin to cover it," Dillon replied. He was sitting on the couch. Lucifer had decided that it was okay to settle in next to him, provided he continued to scratch him behind the ear. "You recognize that guy?"

"I think so. Tough to say with the holes between his eyes. You seem to be developing a pattern here. What the hell happened? Where were you? "

"What happened? The bastard came here to kill me. This wasn't some break-in gone wrong. He came here looking to nail me. I was home all night, reviewing files." Dillon nodded toward the two stacks of files on the coffee table. "As far as going out on the town, I took the dog for a walk around half-past seven. We were gone maybe a half-hour, tops. Then I went back to the files and eventually fell asleep out here." He saw no real need to mention his two-hour investigation of <u>Fifty Shades of Grey</u>.

"The dog growling woke me, and before I could even get up, your boy charged through the front door and into the bedroom, shooting in the dark. I didn't have any other option. He was set on killing me."

"It would certainly seem that way. Where'd the dog come from?"

"My understanding is he belonged to Sinéad."

"How'd he end up back here with you?"

"I found him tied to the doorknob this afternoon with a note. The note is behind you, right there on the table."

McCabe turned and read the note, but he didn't touch it. "The thing's name is Lucifer?" he said and looked over at the two of them.

"Apparently. Don't let his calm demeanor fool you. He's anything but, thank God. If it wasn't for him I'd be in that bed right now looking like a piece of Swiss cheese. Little bastard saved my life." As if on cue the dog sort of half-rolled over, and licked Dillon's hand.

"And you don't know who left him here."

"No idea, but he's staying, that's for damn sure."

"All right. Have you given a statement?"

"No, not officially. I said a few things to the officers as they came in. I told them I was a recent addition to the force. I forget who, exactly, but I know I gave someone your name."

"You phoned this into Emergency Services?"

"No, not that I didn't try. I was calling the US number, we use 911. One of the guys told me it's 999 over here. So I never actually made the call, but I'm guessing a number of people on the floor or in the building did. I heard the first sirens within just a couple of minutes."

McCabe nodded. "I think it would be best if you came down and made a formal statement. The sooner we get that out of the way, the better. I won't be interviewing, whoever is on the night shift will take your statement."

"Can I bring Lucifer?"

"Who?"

Dillon glanced down at Lucifer, snuggled up against his side. "Him, the dog. I don't want to leave him here. Believe me, he'll screw up the scene, and God only knows what else."

"Bring him?" McCabe seemed to think about that for a moment. "I suppose. The way you tell it, sounds like he saved your worthless ass."

"Yeah, he did, thank God. So much for this being a secure building."

McCabe ignored that last comment, and instead said, "Put some shoes on, and grab a jacket it's a bit cool outside."

Dillon carried the dog into the small hallway. The body was still on the floor, exactly where the first responders had found him. The weapon he'd fired, which looked like a sawed-off version of an AK, had bounced when he dropped it and lay up against the closet door. Two individuals in hazmat suits were taking photographs.

McCabe waited in the living room a brief moment and took a casual glance around. He saw the copy of <u>Fifty Shades of Grey</u> sitting on the shelf, but it didn't register. He was too busy wondering if Dillon was going to turn out to be a royal pain in the ass or if he was just what they'd been looking for. Time would tell, he guessed and headed out the door.

* * *

McCabe drove them down to the station. Dillon had tried to put Lucifer in the backseat, but he kept jumping into the front, and after a half-dozen times, McCabe finally gave up and said, "Just hold onto that little wanker. He's driving me crazy, hopping back and forth like that. We don't need the little bastard causing a crash. We've already got enough on our plate for one night."

Dillon gave his statement. McCabe was in the interview room at the time, but he was not the interviewing officer, more like he was there for moral support. Lucifer sat on Dillon's lap during the entire interview, which made Dillon think that once he got a new bed, maybe he would even sleep in it.

Since the apartment was still a crime scene, they put the two of them, Dillon and Lucifer, up in a nearby hotel once the interview was completed. Dillon was allowed to grab a change of clothes and some toiletries at the apartment. McCabe insisted that he bring the files so he would have something to keep him occupied for the remainder of the weekend. He promised to pick Dillon up at half-past eight on Monday morning.

"And be ready, I don't want to waste thirty minutes waiting for the likes of you."

Other than taking Lucifer on three separate walks, Dillon confined himself to the hotel room, spending a number of hours becoming intimately familiar with the files. The two of them, Lucifer and Dillon, dined in the privacy of the hotel room on roast beef, mashed potatoes, red beets, and beer. They fell asleep before ten watching the television. Dillon propped a chair against the door for added security and slept through the night until morning when Lucifer woke him for a walk.

SIXTEEN

McCabe picked him up promptly at nine on Monday morning.

Dillon decided the wiser course would be to not mention he was a half-hour late.

"Where's your friend?" McCabe asked as Dillon slid into the passenger seat and responded with a blank look. "That pain in the ass mutt," McCabe said.

"Oh, yeah, Lucifer. I left him in the room with a note on the door telling them to just work around him."

McCabe rolled his eyes but didn't comment. "Buckle up there. We've got a stop on the way in, Ann Dumphy," he said, then glanced over to see Dillon's reaction. "She asked to see you."

Ann was wounded in the shootout at the airport. She and Dillon had gotten on well. Okay, they'd spent the night in bed together, and the better part of the following afternoon for that matter, although Dillon wasn't about to let McCabe, nor anyone else, know that. He was anxious to see her, but between getting assigned over here, moving into an apartment, an attempt on his life, and Lucifer, he had sort of run out of time. He wondered—

"Did you even hear what I just said? I said we're going to stop and see Ann Dumphy on the way into the office."

Dillon half-shook his head in an effort to return to reality. "Yeah, yeah. Umm, so how's she doing?"

"I think she's doing okay, check that, she's actually doing pretty well, as a matter of fact. She has a good doctor and an excellent nursing staff."

"Is she already out of the hospital?"

McCabe gave him a look that suggested he was nuts. "She took one round in the lung and another one in the shoulder that damn near nicked an artery. It'll be at least six months' recovery, maybe longer, if she can even come back. She might end up on light duty sitting behind a desk for the rest of her career, which would be a shame. She's damn good in the field. Then again, the alternative…" McCabe said, and let that last portion just sort of drift off.

Dillon was having trouble getting the image of Ann lying on the ground out of his head. He'd had his hand pressed over her chest wound. A "sucking chest wound," they'd called it in the army. He kept screaming for a medic, for help, and the God damn time somehow managed to just stand still. His hands seemed to be covered in more and more blood, and he couldn't stop the bleeding. He kept thinking—

"What in the hell is with you, Dildo? Did you even hear what I just said? Come on, get your damn head back in the fecking game."

"Oh, sorry. I was just thinking, the last time I saw her was at the airport, it seemed to take forever before help arrived. God, I just keep picturing her lying there on the ground, and there was nothing I could do."

"Well, don't be too hard on yourself, that's my job, and I truly enjoy it. Come on, you saved her life, along with Bobby Reilly's. You would have been killed, except you shot the bastards first."

McCabe gave a quick glance over at Dillon riding in the passenger seat with a blank look on his face. "Hey, Dildo? Are you okay? You able to deal with seeing her?" His concern sounded genuine.

"What? Oh, yeah, not a problem. In fact, it'll be good for me to see her. And she's doing okay, you said?"

McCabe glanced again, gave Dillon a momentary study, then said, "Let me tell you, that woman puts her mind to something, it's going to get done. Right now, she's thinking recovery and getting back to work. I know her well enough to know she's focused on that, and God help anyone, or anything, that starts to get in her way. If anyone can recover, it's Ann."

"So, you've seen her?"

"I've been checking in on her every day," he said but didn't bother to comment any further. A few minutes later, he took a left turn, drove past the Botanic Gardens, around the bend, and made a right turn through the entrance gate to Bon Secours Hospital. They passed through a parking lot and pulled into a no-parking zone just in front of the hospital doors.

McCabe turned the car off and said, "Come on, let's go." As they stepped out of the car, a woman came out of the hospital. She gave them a disgusted look and headed off toward the parking lot.

"Good lord, can you imagine coming home to that every night?" McCabe said and headed into the building.

Ann Dumphy's room was on the fourth floor at the end of a very long hallway. The doors to the patients' rooms were open, and Dillon counted four beds to a room. All the beds he'd seen appeared to be occupied.

A uniformed officer was seated in a chair outside a room at the far end of the hall. His legs were stretched out as he half-slumped in the chair. As they got closer, Dillon could see he was reading a Harry Potter book.

"How's it going, PJ?" McCabe said as they approached.

"Not a bother, sir. Yous can go on in. She's been all fancied up for you. This your man, the Yank?" he said, nodding with his chin toward Dillon.

"It is."

The guy stood. He looked to be at least six-foot-four, solid in a farm work sort of way, with a thick chest, heavy forearms, and solid upper arms. He held out his hand to Dillon, smiled, and said, "Thanks."

Dillon shook his hand, which felt like he was squeezing a brick. The man gave a firm squeeze back and nodded at McCabe. "He'll do. Paddy Joe," he said, introducing himself. "But everyone calls me PJ. You need anything, or if this plonker misbehaves, you just let me know. I'll get it sorted for you. Go on in. She's been waiting," he said with a smile, then settled back down in his chair and returned to Harry Potter.

McCabe knocked softly on the door, then pushed it open. The room was painted an off-white that looked almost grey, "Cheery" would not have been the first word that came to mind. There were four beds in the room, but Ann's was the only one occupied. She was sitting up in the hospital bed with the blankets neatly turned down to her waist. Three or four pillows propped her up from behind. The bedsheets looked crisp and starched. There was a wall of monitors just behind the bed, but only one of them seemed to be on. A stand with two separate IV bags hanging from it was pushed off to the side and looked to be ready just in case.

She was wearing some sort of flannel top, white with little pinkish flowers that looked like it had been pressed. The sling holding her arm was white. Her hair was brushed, and she had on a slight bit of makeup and some lip gloss. Dillon noticed that her nails were done. A vase of yellow roses sat on the end table next to the bed, and four more flower arrangements rested on the window sill along with what looked like a large stack of get-well cards.

"Are we ready for visitors?" McCabe asked.

As Dillon stepped in behind McCabe, Ann said, "You're a half-hour late." Then she smiled and waved both of them forward.

"Well, I can see your recovery is progressing, and you're returning back to your cantankerous old self," McCabe laughed. "How you doing?"

"Better every day."

"You remember Marshal Dillon, Ann?" McCabe said and sort of laughed.

She smiled at Dillon, and the next thing he knew, he had suddenly pushed McCabe aside, bent over, and kissed her on the forehead. "Ann, I'm so glad…" And then he got all choked up and couldn't speak. He sniffled a couple of times, and then tears were running down all three of their faces.

McCabe cleared his throat first.

Ann started laughing.

"I'm glad I didn't bring any flowers, there'd be nowhere to put them," Dillon said, looking around the room.

"Thanks for everything. Believe me, there's no need for flowers. If it wasn't for you, I'd have flowers all right, but they'd be on my grave."

An awkward silence followed.

"You're here because you're damn good at your job. Right now, your job is to get better and then get back to work," McCabe said. "I don't know if you're aware of this, but Marshal Dillon has graciously agreed to join us."

"So, I've heard," Ann said and gave a genuine smile.

They chatted for fifteen or twenty minutes and were about to leave when a doctor walked in. He was dressed in what seemed to be the prevailing uniform, blue hospital scrubs. He had a stethoscope wrapped around his shoulders. He appeared to be of average height and weight. His dark hair was neatly combed and parted razor-sharp along the right side. Dillon pegged him at mid-thirties.

He stepped along the far side of the bed and asked, "How are we doing today?" Then he took Ann's hand and held it with his right hand and felt her pulse at the wrist with his left.

There was something about her reaction that suggested to Dillon there might be more than just a doctor-patient relationship going on.

"This is Brandon," Ann said once he released her hand. "He's the boss, at least right now."

Brandon smiled, nodded hello, but didn't introduce himself or bother to leave. Just as the thought flashed through Dillon's mind that Ann seemed to be getting tired, McCabe said, "I wish we could stay a bit longer, but we've got to get Dillon settled in the office and see if we can't begin to get some work out of him. Be nice if he could begin to repay us for our gracious hospitality."

Ann nodded and said, "Thank you both for coming. It was wonderful to see you again, Marshal, and thank you. I owe you, big time."

"You just get better so you can show me the ropes and hopefully run interference where McCabe here is concerned."

"Yes, hurry back so you can save me the headache," McCabe said as he tilted his head toward Dillon.

Brandon, the doctor, nodded and gave them a smile, but didn't speak. They made their way out the door, stopped and chatted with PJ in the hall for another minute, then left.

SEVENTEEN

As he pulled away from the no-parking zone McCabe asked, "So, what'd you think?"He seemed oblivious to the scowls from the couple walking past as they looked at the no-parking sign and then the Garda car. The guy growled something to his wife, given the look on his face you really didn't need to read his lips.

"What do I think? I thought she looked great. Tired after twenty minutes, but a week ago, lying on the ground out at terminal two, I wasn't sure she was going to make it. Tell me about your man, PJ."

"PJ? Oh, he's been on for years. Just the sort to be stopping anyone with the idea of paying her a *visit*. Don't let his charming personality fool you."

"How long is he there?"

"Ever since your visitor over the weekend, we've got PJ and another lad pulling shifts. They're each on for twelve hours."

"Long day."

"Necessary evil, unfortunately. Everyone volunteered. It just wouldn't be on if something were to happen to her in there. But I'll feel a lot better when we can get her out of there and home, safe and sound."

"Any idea when that might be?"

"They say she may be going home as early as Wednesday, which under the circumstances is really fast. They just want to check her out for another day or two, hopefully, she'll get the okay, then home. Worst place you can be at some point is in the damn hospital."

"What's with the silent doctor?" Dillon asked.

"Brandon? Bit of the silver lining, I'd say. Ann's rushed in. He's your man on duty, gets her stabilized. Turn's out they had a thing for one another in secondary school. Then, like so many children of the west, they left and went their separate ways only to have him turn up as your man on the front line the day she really needed one. I'd say they're both smitten with one another. He's been in with her just about every time I've paid a visit. Was at her side for many the hour, slept in the chair while she was in that induced coma. I'd have to say, it seems to have paid off."

Dillon thought about that, knew in his heart it was probably the better option both for him and for Ann Dumphy. About all he could ever offer her would be sleepless nights and one hell of a lot of worry.

"… meet everyone and begin to get the lay of the land," McCabe said, then looked over at Dillon and said,

"You look like you're on another planet. Did you hear anything I just said?"

"Yeah, yeah, I heard you. I think it makes a lot of sense."

McCabe gave him another long look but didn't say anything.

They were at the office fifteen minutes later. With all the congestion largely due to the construction on the streets, it seemed more like waiting in traffic than actually driving. Contrary to his actions throughout the rest of the city, McCabe pulled into the parking lot and parked in a space just like everyone else.

They showed their ID's as they passed a security desk, then took the elevator to the third floor. The elevator seemed just large enough to accommodate four people, provided no one was overly large or in the ninth month of pregnancy. Once off the elevator, they walked down to the end of the hall. McCabe held his ID in front of an electronic device on the wall. The door lock clicked open, and McCabe led the way in.

The office consisted of a large room. The walls were painted a depressing battleship grey. Flickering yellow florescent lights strained to illuminate the area. If he had to guess, Dillion would have thought the office was designed to handle eight desks comfortably. He counted sixteen, and a line of file cabinets arranged along one entire wall. Everyone seemed to be working diligently, or was that just because McCabe had suddenly appeared? One of the desks, mounded with mugs, empty paper cups, a couple of dirty plates, stacks of files, and at least two newspapers, appeared to be the collection point for all things discarded.

"We'll be meeting in the conference room in fifteen minutes," McCabe called out to the masses. He pointed to the desk with all the junk piled on it and said, "You can take that one, Dillon. Might as well clear it off and hose it down. Conference room is behind the door marked 'Conference Room.'" With that, he stepped into a corner office and closed the door.

Dillon looked around, suddenly aware of heads turning away and everyone trying to look busy. A guy in shirt sleeves with short dark hair glanced around the office. Once he determined no one was going to come to Dillon's aid, he donned a look of resignation, got up from behind his desk, and walked over.

"Sean Flynn," he said, holding out his hand. They shook hands. He glanced at the trash desk and said, "Because of you, now we have to find a new place to store things. Let me help you with those teacups. Come on, we can dump them in what serves as a break room." He proceeded to grab three ceramic mugs in one hand, a stack of paper cups that looked like they'd come from a coffee machine in the other, and headed past a line of desks. Dillon followed with mugs, cups, and a stack of plates and had the feeling everyone was staring as they passed.

"Just dump those plates and mugs here in the sink. Someone needs one they can wash the damn thing," Flynn said, setting three mugs in the sink. He stepped over to a trashcan and dropped a half-dozen paper cups into it, then half-jumped back when the brown liquid splashed upward. Dillon placed his mugs and plates in the sink, dumped the remnants of tea from the paper cups down the drain, then carefully deposited the cups in the trashcan.

"Come on, I'll copy the list of office extensions for you. You can call the file room and have them collect all that shite stacked up on your desk. Might want to do a quick check while you're at it, seems to be something fouler than usual emanating from that desk. We've all worked at ignoring whatever it is, so you're just in time. I'm guessing either remnants of a leftover meal or a dead rat, that is unless someone, umm, never mind. Let me copy that list for you," he said.

They were standing in front of the copy machine, a piece of office equipment that had to be close to Dillon's age. Something brown had spilled down the front of the machine and stained the grey industrial carpet beneath. Across the top of the machine, a series of metric measurements indicating various lengths of paper ran along one side. Someone had written in indelible marker, "Place Bum Here," with an arrow pointing to the center of the glass screen.

Sean placed a one-page list of extension numbers face down on the copy machine then made a show of pressing the button labeled "Copy" and stepped back. "This'll give you everyone's extension number in the office. Although to tell you the truth, I've found it easier to just yell across the room. Well, that is unless you're trying to get a piece off one of the tarts."

Dillon couldn't tell if he was joking or not.

"Here we are, your own personal list of numbers that no one will answer if you bother to call. Not sure if Inspector McCabe mentioned it, but the file room is actually down the hall and around the corner. This is their extension here," he said, pointing to the number labeled "File Room."

"I'd recommend you call them first, tell them to get their arse in here and clean up that infernal mess on your new desk. Then maybe douse the desk with a gallon or two of disinfectant, or better yet, just set the bloody thing on fire," he said without smiling.

"Four minutes, people," McCabe called as he stepped out of his office, and suddenly, pandemonium seemed to reign as everyone jumped to their feet and hurried past the copy machine toward the break room with empty mugs.

"Shit, already?" Sean said, and hurried back to his desk, leaving Dillon standing at the copy machine, looking at his new list of phone extensions.

"Best grab a mug, Marshal, to help you through the meeting," someone called as they hurried past.

Dillon picked up his list of office extension numbers and hurried into the break room. An electric kettle was making a loud gurgling sound as it came to the boil while two women seemed to be arguing over the last tea bag in the Lipton box.

There was a short line in front of the candy machine as some guy slapped the side of the machine, so the chocolate bar he'd just purchased would drop down off the rack. Another guy was standing in front of the refrigerator, holding an empty package of Oreo cookies, yelling, "What the feck?" to everyone in the room.

EIGHTEEN

McCabe glanced around, cleared his throat, and said, "All right, quiet down, let's get this over with. Flynn, did you hear what the hell I just said?"

"No, sorry, boss, I was busy talking. Could you repeat it?" Everyone chuckled, including McCabe then the room gradually settled down.

There were a dozen chairs around a conference table, all filled. Three guys leaned against a white radiator along one wall. McCabe stood in a corner next to a whiteboard. Two women leaned against the wall behind him. Just about everyone, except Dillon, was sipping tea. A few of the mugs looked like the ones he and Sean had placed in the break room sink not five minutes ago.

"Quick update, for those of you who haven't had the opportunity to meet the latest addition to our staff. I'd like to present Marshal Jack Dillon, late of the US. He is now officially on board, so please be patient." This last line brought a few chuckles and smiles throughout the room.

"Marshal Dillon and I stopped by to see Ann Dumphy this morning. I'm happy to report that she continues to improve."

"Any idea when she'll be out?" a woman behind McCabe asked. Her tone in the brief question suggested she was a no-nonsense sort. As if the tone wasn't enough, she had a scar along the left side of her face that ran a good four inches from the corner of her mouth up across her cheekbone. The top of her left ear was missing, cut off in a straight line. Dillon's initial assessment was she seemed devoid of any humor, but then factoring in the visible scars he reassessed, and decided she'd maybe been around the block more than once.

"We're hoping soon, Mora. No one is more anxious than Ann. Once she's out of the hospital, we'll leave the decision of when and if she returns up to her. For the moment, let's just be thankful she's on the mend. If I had to hazard a guess, I'd say a minimum of three or four months' additional recovery at home."

Two more women hurried into the room. They were the same two who'd been arguing over the teabag. They must have worked something out because they both carried steaming mugs.

"For those of you who have not had the pleasure," McCabe said, staring at the two, "I've already noted the presence of Marshal Jack Dillon, of late from the States. Jack will be joining us for an oh, undetermined amount of time. We had an incident this past weekend that I'm sure you're all aware of. It seems someone disturbed the sleep of Jack's dog."

At this point, McCabe opened a manila file folder on the table, grabbed a sheaf of papers, and handed them to the guy seated closest to him. Dillon could just make out the image of an individual in the upper left-hand corner of the handout.

"Take one and pass them on. This is the information on one Borya Fedorov, age twenty. Apparently entered the EU illegally, we're not sure when or for that matter where. No idea when or how he arrived in Ireland. No idea at this stage where he resided. He is the first of the three gunmen from last week's terminal two incident that we've been able to identify. Any additional information you might come across would be greatly appreciated. Questions?"

"Follow up on body reclamation?" one of the guys leaning against the radiator asked.

"About all I can tell you is that as of the close of business yesterday, no one either here or outside the EU has made an inquiry. But it's still early, let's see what happens."

"Weapons trace?" This from O'Malley, who was leaning against the doorframe, apparently another late arrival.

"Standard, AK-74's, two shooters, appear to each have had a thirty-round magazine in their possession. All the magazines were the steel-reinforced plastic versions. Where and how they came in possession of the weapons and ammunition remains an unknown. The driver of the vehicle was armed with a nine-millimeter Makarov pistol. No serial numbers. Estimates are it was manufactured prior to 1991, again, as of this time, we are unable to determine where, when, and how it ended up in his possession."

"What was your man armed with Saturday night?"

"Another AK-74, with a thirty-round magazine. The magazine appears to be similar to those recovered at terminal two. The weapon from Saturday night was modified to eliminate the shoulder stock, and Dermot, did you get a clarification?" McCabe asked.

A dark-haired guy with glasses standing at the back of the room took a half-step forward. "The weapon was originally manufactured for Soviet airborne troops sometime prior to 1991. This make was originally manufactured with a folding stock. The current theory is the stock was removed for ease of transport, and, well, it just makes it that much easier to hide the damn thing."

McCabe nodded, looked around the room for further questions or comments. "As a side note to Saturday night, security cameras at the corner captured a 2012 KIA Ceed racing through a stoplight at the corner. Time coincides with our incident. Color is light blue or green. It may have been involved. A vehicle was heard speeding away just after the shooter had been subdued. Just to keep things interesting, there's no license information. Still, a bit of knowledge to tuck away. Questions?"

No one said anything.

"Last bit of info, as I started out to say, some of you have already met Jack Dillon. Over the course of the next few weeks, please take a moment and introduce yourselves. We'll be working to integrate him into our, mmm-mmm, efforts. Okay, thank you. Let's get back to work."

With that, everyone got up and filed out of the room. The woman with the scarred cheek held back until most of the crowd had left the room. She extended a hand, smiled, and said, "I'm Mora. Pleased to meet you. If I can help you getting settled, let me know. We're all doing the work of three, so it's a bit crazy finding the time, but folks will come round. Don't be afraid to ask."

"Nice to meet you, Mora," Dillon said. He tried not to study the scar across her cheek, but couldn't help it. It appeared to be perfectly in line with the missing top of her left ear, and he thought it a safe bet that she had literally dodged a bullet. She smiled at him, then picked up her tea mug and left the room. Just McCabe and Dillon remained in the conference room.

"Questions?" McCabe asked.

"No, pretty short and to the point. I like that. I've never been much of a meeting person."

McCabe nodded, closed his manila folder, and began to head for the door.

"There is one thing," Dillon said, causing him to stop just as he was about to leave the room.

"Oh?"

"What would it take to get a coffee pot in here? It looks like everyone drinks tea around this office."

"Not a problem, Marshal Dillon. Just go out and buy yourself one, well, and the coffee, too. Anything else?"

"No, that should just about do it."

NINETEEN

It took three calls before someone answered the phone in the file room. Whoever it was didn't seem too happy with Dillon's request to get the files off his desk. In the end, they promised to get there sometime during the day. In the meantime, Dillon deposited two more tea mugs in the break room sink. He guessed they were abandoned on what was now his desk as people filed out of the conference room, but he couldn't be sure. It took the better part of a half-hour, but he managed to remove all the files off the desk and neatly stack them on top of the filing cabinets lining the far wall.

With the top of the desk cleared off, he began going through drawers. It became immediately apparent that Sean Flynn had been right, there was something foul about the desk area. He found the problem in the bottom drawer. It was either really old beef or over-cooked chicken festering in a bowl with a spoon. He couldn't be sure of the contents, and he really didn't want to risk further investigation. Whatever it was, the concoction had taken on a life of its own and looked to be growing, literally. He hauled the dish into the break room, found a discarded plastic bag from Eurospar, placed the dish with the spoon inside the bag, knotted the bag, and placed it in the trash bin. Then he thoroughly washed his hands, twice, using hot water and lots of soap.

When he returned, someone had placed a spray bottle of cleaning solution and a roll of paper towels on the desk. Everyone suddenly appeared to be so diligently at work that they didn't have the time to even glance in his direction. He sprayed down everything and wiped it clean, twice, then turned his attention to the drawer that held the science experiment and began the first of three treatments.

Thirty minutes later, a pudgy guy with a shirttail hanging out, a loosened tie, and a ruddy face arrived with a four-wheel cart. Dillon had just finished his final go-through on the bottom drawer with the cleaning solution.

"You the one who called about a file to return?"

"A file? As in one? No. There are a bunch of files that need to be returned. I stacked them along the top of the file cabinet over there."

He turned, looked, then mumbled, "Feck's sake," and gave Dillon a look.

"Don't blame me. This is my first day. Those files are just part of what was piled on this desk. You wouldn't believe what was inside it."

"Oh yeah, this desk, I remember now. This is, well, I guess, *was* the trash desk. Hey, you ever find out what was smelling so bad?"

He was about to say something when McCabe stuck his head out of the office door. "Dillon, you got a minute?"

He smiled at the file guy and said, "Gee, sorry, I was really looking forward to giving you a hand, but, well, you just heard."

The look he got in response suggested he wasn't buying it.

TWENTY

McCabe looked up as Dillon entered his office. "Did you get rid of whatever died in that desk?"

"Yeah, I dumped it in some sort of hazardous waste container."

"Better make sure your shot record is up-to-date," he said, then closed the door behind him. O'Malley was seated on a couch along with Mora, the woman with the scarred face he'd met just a little earlier. "Grab a seat," McCabe said and indicated a chair opposite his desk, then walked behind the desk and settled into a large, black leather throne.

It was the first time Dillon had actually been in McCabe's office. The walls were bare with the exception of three framed photos, two guys and a woman, all in uniform. Each frame had a strip of black cloth hanging across the upper right-hand corner of the frame, signifying the individuals were dead. Killed in the line of duty, Dillon guessed but didn't feel the time was necessarily right to ask about it.

"Are you two filing a complaint against me?" he asked O'Malley and Mora.

"I was thinking about it," O'Malley said, "but the list of charges would be so long—"

"Besides," Mora said. "Ever since you removed that dead rat or whatever it was from your desk today, things have actually improved in the office, so maybe we'll just call it even."

"I hate to interrupt, but maybe we could get down to business," McCabe said. He rested his elbows on his desk and leaned forward. "Here's the thing, Dillon. We've picked up some fairly strong rumors that suggest there's a price on your head. For one thing…"

"A price on my head? By who? What the hell did I do?"

"Well, for starters, you shot and killed three gang members out at terminal two just a little more than a week ago. Then your late-night visitor on Saturday night was wheeled out in a body bag. You start putting all this together, and it would seem you've become a bit of a problem for our Russian friends."

"Maybe if they'd stop trying to kill me," Dillon said without a trace of humor.

"Here's what we're picking up. After the last two incidents, you're starting to make them look rather foolish. In fact, you're beginning to make it look like they can't take care of their own, making it appear as though they're not up to the task of dealing with one little old trouble-maker."

"Watch how you use that term 'old,'" Dillon said.

All three of them smiled, then Mora said, "My informants tell me there's been quite a bit of, umm, how can I phrase it? 'Behind the scenes chatter' suggesting the people in charge might be losing their grip."

"And just who would that be?" Dillon asked.

"The name Alexei Bazanov ring any bells?" O'Malley said.

"Well, yeah. I mean, it rings some bells because I spent the last three days of my life reviewing the files you left me. I recognize the name, know he lives on the south side of Dublin…."

"Dub 4," O'Malley said.

"His name keeps popping up as a person of interest, and I'd guess if things here are anything like the States, he's got a platoon of lawyers who follow him around and somehow manage to keep him at arm's length from any connection to the actual crimes he's responsible for."

"It would appear he's put a price on your head," McCabe said.

"Let's be honest. I was just in the wrong place at the wrong time. The last thing I need is to become a problem for some group of morally deficient psychotics. I didn't go out to the damn airport with the intent of killing someone. I was just going to transport a prisoner back to the States."

"Ackermann, a prisoner who, apparently, had a good deal of inside knowledge when it came to Bazanov."

"But I didn't know that."

"Really not the point, Jack. Unfortunately, that's the reality just now, and sorry to say, they simply aren't very interested in knowing your side of the story. You've become a major pain in the arse for these folks. That said, we're thinking there just might be an opportunity to use this to our advantage."

"Use it to your advantage?"

"Our advantage," McCabe said, sort of encompassing everyone in the room before he looked Dillon in the eye. "You're one of us now. Especially since you cleaned out that desk." They all laughed for a moment. It struck Dillon as a bit of forced laughter. He smiled and waited for the other shoe to drop.

"There are a couple of things we have to do. First off, unfortunately, we're going to have to move you again. The possibility of collateral damage is simply too great where you are."

"Exactly where can I go that my presence won't be a factor?"

McCabe shot O'Malley a look.

"Well, it so happens that we have a very nice property just outside of Dublin," O'Malley said.

"A farm in the Dublin Mountains. Gorgeous area," Mora added. "Walking paths nearby, beautiful scenery."

"I got some psychotic Russian gangster out there who's put a price on my head, and you're thinking it might be a good idea if I take a walk in the mountains?"

"It's remote, about the only collateral damage would be to some nearby sheep," O'Malley chuckled.

"Oh, well, now that makes me feel a lot better," Dillon said.

"We can spread the rumor that you're out there, basically in hiding. See if we can't get some of them to show themselves, try something, then, once we capture them, we'll have new access to information," McCabe said.

"Access to infor— Define 'try something.'"

"Well, we expect they're going to attempt to try and kill you again," McCabe said.

"Gee, don't sugarcoat it. It sounds like you're setting me up to be something like a helpless lamb out there, tied to a stake. What's my job? Just sit there and pray to God they're lousy shots? Hope they aren't successful in getting to me?"

"Something like that. Only we'll have a team embedded, ready, and able to deal with any situation."

"Deal with any situation?"

"At least we think so," O'Malley said.

"Think so? Gee, pardon me for not feeling all that comfortable with that last response. Just a couple of scenarios here. What would happen if, for example, they launched a drone with a bomb? Or, I'm guessing there's a water well, what happens if they poisoned the well? Or hey, maybe just set the place on fire and shoot me when I run outside?"

"I didn't mean to suggest there isn't a certain element of danger here. But the fact is…"

"Element of danger? Are you kidding? The whole idea sounds damn near suicidal. The fact is, the way it sounds, I'd have to be completely nuts to even think about going through with this."

"So you're not willing to take part, is that it?"

"No, I didn't say that. I just want to look at the various options is all. I mean, yeah, count me in. Let's do it. I just don't want to be surprised at the last minute."

There seemed to be a palpable sigh of relief coming from the couch.

"Good. We'll move you in tonight and spread the word once you're settled. Essentially, the plan is to have you surrounded by four two-person teams, eight officers altogether. You'll be given two devices for contact, one primary, one backup. You'll be armed, have a protective vest, a vehicle, food for a week, and a safe room. Any questions?"

"Can I bring Lucifer?"

"Lucifer?" McCabe asked, clearly not making the connection.

"That fecking dog?" O'Malley said, sounding disgusted.

"The little black one," Mora added.

McCabe shook his head, then said, "Yes, yes, of course, you can bring Lucifer. Why the hell not?"

"Good, then let's get started," Dillon said.

TWENTY-ONE

It was about a forty-five-minute drive from the office to the location in the Dublin Mountains. First, they picked up Dillon's suitcase along with Lucifer. Then, just as he thought they were getting underway, they stopped at a small warehouse. He had the distinct feeling the place wasn't exactly legitimate.

McCabe pulled in front of an unadorned office front and parked. Inside was a small room with a low sort of counter blocking access to a rear door. The room could have been some sort of retail facility in another lifetime except that it was so small it was nearly impossible to imagine what the product line would have been.

The woman behind the counter looked up from her tabloid article on the divorce of a B-grade TV star no one had ever heard of and said, "Your boxes are next to the rear door, one of yas should drive round the back. You can fit your man for the vest inside." She waved Dillon and O'Malley through the door behind her with a jerk of her thumb, while McCabe stepped back outside and drove the car around to the rear of the building.

Dillon and O'Malley stepped into a large warehouse sort of room that smelled of mothballs and wet canvas.

O'Malley led the way through a maze of aisles until they stopped in front of a section of rickety metal shelves. He studied the folded items piled on the middle shelf for a moment, then sorted through a number of them before he grabbed one and held it up.

"Here, try this one on for size."

An IOTV vest, an Improved Outer Tactical Vest. A bulletproof vest in civilian terms, complete with a universal camouflage pattern and some ceramic panels to insert for added protection.

O'Malley helped Dillon fit the vest on. He studied him from the front, back, and side. Pulled at the velcro straps, grabbed the padded shoulders, and shoved Dillon first left and then right before he declared his choice acceptable.

In the meantime, McCabe had pulled the vehicle around to the back, where they loaded three large, heavy boxes into the rear of the car. He went back into the front office, consummated the deal with nothing more than a signature, and thirty minutes later, they were headed into the Dublin Mountains.

Lucifer was sitting next to Dillon in the backseat, contentedly positioned on top of a number of rain poncho's and the IOTV. He was gazing out the windows, looking for all the world like an emperor on parade.

"So where in the hell are we going, exactly?" Dillon asked.

O'Malley glanced over at McCabe and smiled.

"Not far off the mark, actually. We're headed for Hellfire."

"Hell what?"

"Hellfire. Never heard of it?"

"No, not really."

"Oh, God, well, let's see. Famous locally, it was originally an old Neolithic cairn. Some rich bastard purchased the land back in the seventeen-forties, I think. Used the stone from the cairn to build a summer home or a hunting lodge or some damn thing. Later on, it was purchased by a number of worthless wealthy bastards, presumably to meet with the devil, but more likely to just sit around, get shit-faced, and, with any luck, screwed by the local wenches."

"You gotta be kidding. This is the place where you're going to set me up as a target?"

"Oh, no, well, that is, not exactly. It's just nearby, Hellfire is. No, not to worry, you're going to be comfortably situated in the Connolly Farm, a charming, rustic cottage we acquired a few years back."

"And where are the Connollys?"

"Hard to say, exactly…."

"Well, we know that plonker Peter is in prison," O'Malley said.

"Oh, yeah, of course. I think for another seven or eight years?" McCabe looked over at O'Malley.

"Tax evasion, illegal cigarettes, a bit of the firearms network."

McCabe nodded. "At the end of the investigation, once he got the message that he was going to do some serious time, he was suddenly able to give us quite a bit of information. When was it, Pat, two, three years ago? God, for the life of me, it seems like only yesterday."

"Afraid it was more like four years by now. Course, his wife—"

"Ahhh, the lovely Laura, God knows where she's off to. They told us France, but I've always suspected the south of Spain."

"She got off, got away?" Dillon asked.

"More or less. As it turns out, she was the one who actually blew the whistle on the old man, her husband, Peter. Seems he had a thing for a younger one."

"More than one younger one," O'Malley laughed. "God, the poor bastard couldn't keep it in his pants."

"Not a happy bunny when he learned what she'd done, but by that time it was too late. He was under lock and key, and she just up and disappeared," McCabe said.

O'Malley half-turned and looked at Dillon in the back seat. "Far as we know, she made some sort of deal with the higher-ups and apparently left the country. No other way she could have disappeared into thin air like that. Good riddance to the two of 'em, I say. Country's better off with 'em either locked up or just gone, and to hell with the pair of them."

"And so you got their farm?"

"The service did, in a way. Once you see the place and you know what your man did to make a few quid, it'll all makes sense." At that point, they crossed a narrow stone bridge. McCabe slowed and took a right-hand turn.

The paved road he cautiously pulled onto was more a trail than a road, and barely the width of a small driveway. Neither side of the road had a shoulder. Stone walls and hedges ran along both sides, and God only knew what you'd do if you met an oncoming car. Thankfully they didn't meet anyone.

McCabe stopped the car at a dirt road, and O'Malley hurried out to open a rusty gate attached to two brick pillars that looked like they were ready to fall down. Once open, they pulled ahead, and the gate gave a loud groan as O'Malley pulled it closed again. They drove down a rutted dirt road that appeared not to have seen traffic in quite some time and headed toward a grey, two-story structure in the distance.

The structure was actually a house made of stone with a slate roof. The windows and front door sported peeling white paint. Dillon remembered O'Malley's comment about Connolly having been in jail for the past four years. The place looked like it hadn't seen very much activity, and certainly no maintenance, in all that time. Lace curtains hung in all the windows, but through the dirty glass, the lace looked yellowed and grey. A small tree had apparently taken root in the mortar of one of the chimneys, and a sapling, maybe three feet tall, stretched up above the top of the chimney— all in all, not the warmest-looking place to come home to.

Remnants of a smaller structure were attached to the east side of the house at an angle. A rusted sheet metal roof had collapsed some time ago and lay more or less inverted within the stone walls. The upper portion of the far wall had fallen in on top of the sheet metal. Dillon guessed at one time the place may have served as a small barn, or maybe a tool shed, although it now appeared to be beyond repair.

"Home sweet home," McCabe said as he pulled in front of the door. He turned the car off, and they all sat for a moment, staring, no one saying anything before climbing out.

There was a small window set in the upper half of the front door. A soiled lace curtain hung over the window. The glass appeared too dirty to see inside. Once Dillon opened the rear door, Lucifer ran over to the structure with the collapsed roof, lifted his leg, and relieved himself against the wall.

Dillon stood next to the car and looked around. A large open field, maybe a hundred yards long, lay in front of the structure and ran back out to what passed as the road. The field was edged with a rusty barbed wire fence, either down or broken in a number of places. A patch of foot-high grass ran out to an overgrown hedge along the far side of the house. What looked like a dilapidated outhouse appeared to be getting slowly taken over by the hedge.

"You've got to be kidding me. Please don't tell me this place doesn't have indoor plumbing?"

McCabe was in the process of unlocking the front door. He fumbled with a small set of keys until he found the right one. It had taken him three tries.

"Don't you worry about it. Come on, Dildo, take a look inside, your palace awaits," he said, and stepped into the small front hall. Dillon stepped in behind him just as McCabe stomped his feet a couple of times, and they suddenly heard small creatures scurrying around inside the walls. "Well, at least it sounds like you won't be alone. Nice and cozy, don't you think?"

There was a definite chill to the place, which probably accounted for the overwhelming musty smell. Off to the left of the entry was what Dillon would have thought of as the living room. The well-worn floor appeared to be made of pine, and the room was completely empty, devoid of anything resembling furniture. There was a fireplace on one wall with a pile of ashes below the grate and an empty whiskey bottle on the rough, sawn timber that served as a mantel. A large, white plastic bag leaned against the wall next to the fireplace. McCabe walked over, pulled the top of the bag open, and peeked inside.

"Oh, grand, more than enough turf for the night. Too bad there's not a chair to sit on in here, you might have found it comfortable," he said. Then he walked out of the room and into the kitchen. Dillon followed just as a mouse scurried across the floor and wiggled through a knothole in the mopboard.

The kitchen featured a large fireplace, easily twice the size of the one in the living room, with an iron bar that swung in and out with a pot hanging from it. Off to the left along the wall were some rough-looking cabinets with a wooden countertop, and next to the cabinets, in the back corner, an antique refrigerator.

McCabe walked over to the refrigerator and opened the door. "Damnit, the stupid bastards were supposed to plug it in. Well, say a prayer," he said, then took the electric cord on the refrigerator and plugged it into a wall socket just above the kitchen counter. The socket sparked and McCabe jumped back, shaking his hand, but the light came on in the refrigerator. A moment later, the thing started to hum, and he closed the door. "There, problem solved."

"Let's bring everything in here, get you somewhat settled before we give you a tour of the place upstairs," he said. They hauled the three boxes along with Dillon's bulletproof vest and the poncho's into the empty living room and set them in the middle of the floor.

Dillon went back outside and had to call Lucifer a half-dozen times before the little guy made his way out of the rubble of the attached structure. He came out carrying a small doll in his mouth, which he promptly walked over and dropped at Dillon's feet.

"No offense, Lucifer, but that is really warped. A doll, really?"

"Lucifer looked up at him with mournful eyes."

"Oh, God, all right, all right," he said. "But just this once." Then he turned to make sure McCabe wasn't watching, picked up the doll and tossed it into the dark.

Lucifer took off after it, searched in weeds tall enough that Dillon was unable to see where he was, and then, just as Dillon was about to whistle, Lucifer returned with the doll. Dillon took the doll, egged Lucifer into the front door then tossed the doll back into the pile of rubble.

TWENTY-TWO

Once Lucifer was back inside, McCabe said, "Let's check out the upstairs," and with that, he headed up the rickety staircase. Dillon followed. Lucifer was busy in the kitchen, sniffing around various corners, and the refrigerator for God only knew what.

O'Malley stood at the base of the stairs and said, "One note of caution. Best not to depend on this railing for much." Then he grabbed hold and shook the railing three or four inches from side to side to prove his point.

"All the windows in the house have built-in shutters," McCabe said from the top of the stairs. He turned and stepped into the bedroom, positioned directly above the empty living room on the first floor. It was a good-sized room, for a bedroom, with what looked like a king-sized bed. Clean, folded linens and blankets were neatly arranged on the corner of the bed. There was a fireplace on one wall, directly above the one in the living room. Just like the room below it, the bare wood floor was worn. With the exception of the bed, the room was completely devoid of any furniture. The only place to sit was on the bed.

"The shutters in here, well actually throughout the entire house were designed to look like wood panels, but they're actually half-inch steel," McCabe said, then rapped his knuckles against the shutters and got a solid sound in return. "They'll stop just about any ordnance, short of a rocket-propelled grenade. The walls are a foot and a half thick, and solid stone. Connolly had them steel-reinforced about ten years ago. That front door downstairs has a half-inch of steel on the backside. You play it careful and no one's going to be able to hide in the bushes and take a pot shot at you."

"The place is sort of like a fortress," Dillon said.

"Thanks to Peter Connolly. I'll tell you, you wouldn't believe it now, but in its heyday, it was quite the place. Thick oriental rugs covered the floors. Comfortable, antique furniture, and in the cold months, the Connollys jetted away to Spain or Cuba or the Canaries. The bastards lived the life. I'll give 'em that much. At least they did for a while. Come on, let me show you the bath," he said and left Dillon standing in the bedroom, staring at the half-inch steel shutters covering the windows, trying to imagine the place with exotic rugs and antique furniture. "You coming, Dildo?"

Dillon stepped out of the bedroom and stood next to McCabe, wearing a large smile. "Now, just so it won't be all bad," McCabe said, then reached for the chrome knob and opened the door. The door squeaked on its hinges as McCabe pushed it open. He took a step back and let Dillon enter.

"Oh! Thank God," Dillon exclaimed. "Indoor plumbing. I can't believe it. God, but you had me going there for a while."

McCabe laughed. "I know the feeling. I've lost count of the people we've had here who looked at that rickety old outhouse in the middle of the overgrown hedge, and you could watch the color begin to drain away from their faces. You've Laura Connolly to thank for this little gem. Originally this was probably two rooms, but the lovely Laura liked her pleasure," he laughed.

The bathroom was made up of alternating black and white marble tiles on the floor. All the walls were white marble with maybe a ten-inch ribbon of smaller black and white tiles running around the entire room at a height of about five feet.

A black marble top with two sink basins sat on top of a white vanity opposite the door. A large mirror with a silver frame covered the entire wall above the vanity. A toilet, bidet, large shower, and then a triangular-shaped tub large enough for two, with whirlpool jets on the side, made up the rest of the room.

"You're kidding me. I would have never guessed this from the outside. It's well, wow."

"Like I said, the lovely Laura liked her pleasure. Of course, behind the marble is another half-inch of steel plating on the exterior walls. Come on, we'll go back downstairs," McCabe said. He stepped out of the bath-room and headed down the staircase. Dillon took a final look around, breathed a sigh of relief, and made a mental note to try the tub with the whirlpool jets later.

McCabe turned halfway down the stairs and looked up at Dillon. "Now, Dildo, you'll note these stairs creak. Loudly. That's by design. Anyone somehow gets in here, believe me, you'll hear the bastards coming before they have half a chance of getting to you. Now I want you to check this out," he said, turning into the kitchen.

He walked across the room toward a tall cabinet next to the fireplace and pulled the cabinet door open. The cabinet was empty. McCabe gave Dillon a quick glance over his shoulder, smiled, then pushed the back of the cabinet. It sprung open, revealing lights shining in the room behind it.

"Come on," he said, stepping into the cabinet and then down a couple of steps.

The room was compact, with a small desk pushed against the far wall. O'Malley was seated at the desk, clicking keys on a keyboard. A half-dozen illuminated screens were mounted on the wall in front of him, showing live images of the area outside. "This is where Connolly stored all his merchandise. Everything in order, Pat?"

"Three-hundred-and-sixty-degree coverage," O'Malley said, then turned toward Dillon. "The system works off its own generator, so no matter what happens, you can still watch things from in here."

"The entire house is wired to a backup generator and battery. Power is ever cut, it should fire back up within sixty seconds."

"Is this an extension on the house?" Dillon asked, then looked around the small room and tried to get his bearings.

"In a manner of speaking. That barn rubble you saw alongside the house, it's actually directly over this area. Connolly had an incident some years back and put in this safe room. There's a phone line that runs underground for the better part of a half-mile so it can't be cut. Course, that was before cellphones. Still, nice and all to have the backup."

"And this house just sits here, empty, like this?"

"For a good part of the time. It's used on what you might call a 'need-to-know' basis. It's served as a safe house from time to time. We've kept the occasional informant in here until we've moved them out of the country. Two of your embassy staff were here about a year ago following an incident. It works best when we can keep traffic to a minimum. Obviously, we don't like to advertise the fact that we have it."

"What if Connolly talks?"

"Then he'll serve an even longer sentence. Truth is after his wife Laura gave us all sorts of information, Connolly is pretty much in solitary confinement, at his request. There's been a price on his head since the day he was incarcerated. So, tell me, Dildo. How are you at cooking dinner?"

TWENTY-THREE

O'Malley stuffed the last bit into his mouth, followed by a final piece of roast potato. "Not a bad job on the steaks,"

Over dinner, they'd been going over the working of the monitoring and communication systems for the umpteenth time until Dillon felt like his eyes were about ready to start spinning in opposite directions.

"The security teams will be arriving around four this morning in two cars," McCabe said. "We'll leave one car here for you. Pat and I will drive the other two cars back into town. I want to have everyone in place before sunrise. You'll go to the grocery store and the wine store tomorrow morning. Stop in at the post office the following day. Maybe show your face a bit at Bulger's, the local pub, in the evening, just to let people know you're here. Chat people up, tell them you're here for a few days. They don't need to know your name, but once they hear you talk, they'll know you're an American. Word will get out."

"What if the bad guys show up while I'm gone?"

"I think that would be pretty unlikely, but if they do, we'll be ready for them, and we can always text or call you on your cell. It's more likely they'll attempt to surprise you in the middle of the night, at least that seems to have been their pattern so far. I want to have you seen in town a couple of times, just in case they have someone poking around and asking questions. We're putting the word out tonight through informants that you've gone into hiding, and you're being sent back to the US in a few days. So, if they're going to act, it will have to be in the next seventy-two hours. Otherwise, they'll be flat out of luck."

"What do you think the chances are they'd try something at the airport?"

"Just about zero. As far as they know, you won't be traveling from Dublin Airport. You'll be flying out of a military airbase, either here or up north. Under the circumstances, they wouldn't find that too unusual. No, if they're going to go for you, it will almost certainly be here."

"You think they'll do it?"

"Hate can be a big motivator," McCabe said.

Dillon was in bed at eleven. On the advice of McCabe, he left all the windows unshuttered in the hopes that some of the locals might be passing down the lane and take notice of the lights on in the house. Word travels faster than most people think in rural areas.

O'Malley knocked on the bedroom door a few hours later and said, "Best get up. Your security team is pulling in. Might as well come on down and meet them before we get them situated. Once they're in place, McCabe and I will be pulling out of here."

Dillon was downstairs a minute later. McCabe and O'Malley were out in front of the house, talking to two men. The four of them were watching as another vehicle, a van, drove in through the front gate, and then headed up toward the house. It took a moment with the camouflage outfit for Dillon to recognize Sean Flynn from the office talking to McCabe off to the side.

"Oh, well look, if it isn't the star of the show," Flynn said as Dillon stepped outside. "All ready to play your part?"

"As ready as I'll ever be. Good to see you, Sean."

"All right, Marshal," McCabe said. "Pat will go over the locations with you on the monitors while we get them settled in. We'll do a quick communications check with each team, and then the two of us are out of here. Are there any last-minute questions you have?"

"No, I'm feeling pretty comfortable. Three days you said?"

"Yeah, seventy-two hours, if they don't make a move by then, they're not going to, and we'll pull everyone. There's always that outside chance they'll just be glad to see the backside of you, but I have trouble with them just letting you fly back to the States. Rumors we're hearing are that they feel they've simply got to be seen making a move on the likes of you."

The van pulled up in front of the house, six guys got out and stretched and groaned. From the groans, you'd swear they'd been driving for hours instead of forty-five minutes. Everyone looked familiar from the conference room meeting yesterday. Even though McCabe introduced him all around, Dillon still wasn't able to remember names. Everyone on the security team referred to him as 'Dildo," which was just fine with Dillon, just as long as they kept the Russians away.

O'Malley took him back into the safe room, and they watched on the monitors as the teams got into position. Once they were in position, O'Malley had Dillon contact each team to check communications. Everything seemed to work. Soon after that, the two of them, O'Malley and McCabe, wished everyone luck, climbed in their respective vehicles and drove away. Dillon stared out across the open field long after they disappeared from sight.

He went back to bed and thought he'd slept fitfully only to wake up from a sound sleep when his cellphone rang.

"Dillon," he answered.

The inside shutters on the windows had remained open overnight, and bright sun was streaming into the room. Bits of dust in the air sparkled in what sunlight managed to stream through the dirty windows.

"Just checking in, Dildo. Anything?" O'Malley asked.

"Not a thing, but then again, it's awfully early. You put the word out?"

"As of late last night, but that's really Mora's gig. You check the monitors this morning?"

"Not yet. I was just about to when you called," Dillon said, slowly getting out of bed and rolling his shoulders to get the kinks out. The left shoulder, where he had been wounded, still felt a little stiff in the morning.

He glanced out the bedroom window. It was a clear day, at least for the moment. His limited experience had taught him that Dublin weather could change in a minute. "You hear a forecast for today?" he asked O'Malley.

"It's supposed to rain later. Wouldn't want to be one of your pals out there, lying in the mud and muck while you're inside, all nice and dry and warm. I'd say you just might be in for more than a few rounds at a pub once this is all over."

"I'll be more than glad to buy if we can get these bastards."

"That is the ultimate prize, ain't it? Get one of 'em and have him sing for his supper. You downstairs yet?"

"Almost. Mind if I run to the bathroom first?"

"Tell you what, do that, get the monitors fired up, then call me back. I got more to do than sitting here listening to you in the loo."

Dillon was back to him in less than ten minutes with the monitors up and running.

"That was fast. I trust you washed your hands."

"No, just wiped 'em clean on the lace curtains."

"That'll really get you sick," he laughed. "You got those monitors on?"

"I do. I'm looking at all four areas. I can't see any-one."

"That's as it should be. Give them each a call, check-in. I want to hear their voices, but don't let on I'm listening in."

Dillon went through the drill, called each team, wished them a good morning, and told them he would be buying rounds once this was all over. No one seemed to put up a fight on that last point.

After he contacted all four posts, O'Malley said, "We want you to go to the petrol station and the grocery store in Ballyboden this morning. Pick up dinner-makings for yourself and whatever you want for lunch. Don't buy too much, because you'll be going back tomorrow and doing more of the same."

"Should I pick something up for the guys?"

"For the…no. You're to stay away from them. Far away. The only contact you're to have is first thing in the morning, last thing in the evening. That's all. They hauled in Defense Force ration packs, so they're taken care of."

Gee, ration packs, Dillon guessed a version of army MREs, meals ready to eat. They'd probably have some fairly cranky guys out there after three days of lying in the mud and eating that stuff. "Anything else? Other-wise, I want to do a couple of things around the place to make it look like someone's here."

"Like what, exactly?"

"I saw a clothes-line out back, I was going to hang a couple of t-shirts out, maybe a towel hanging out the bedroom window. There's a trash bin out front. I was just going to leave the lid open, make it look, I don't know, I guess careless. I was planning to burn some turf in the fireplace later this afternoon and get some smoke coming out of the chimney."

"Good idea. Don't forget, into town around noon and make a couple of purchases."

"Do I need to tell anyone where I'm staying?"

"No, in fact maybe be vague, you know, say 'just around' or 'nearby'. With your American accent, it'll be all over by the end of the lunch hour. Maybe grab a pint or two at the local pub tonight. Not too late, we want you home by nine. Oh, and one more thing."

"Yeah?"

"Mind yourself, Dillon. Be careful."

TWENTY-FOUR

I rish lunchtime seemed to be closer to one o'clock, so Dillon headed into the village of Ballyboden about half-past eleven. If he'd been driving any faster, he would have missed the village completely. Fortunately, there was a stoplight that caught his attention, and he pulled into the small parking area that accommodated the store. He talked to the woman behind the meat counter, mentioned to her he was staying nearby for a day or two and picked out a steak.

He told the cashier the same thing and asked her where the nearest petrol station was. She looked at him for a long moment, then pointed out the window, directly across the street, to a Topaz service station with eight pumps. "Can't get much closer than that," she said.

He bought a bottle of wine at a shop called O'Brien's, told the guy he was staying nearby and asked if he could recommend any hiking trails. The conversation went on for fifteen minutes, covering three different trails, each two to three hours long, going through the Dublin Mountains. He was back at the Connolly farm a little before two. He left the rusted gate open and parked the car out front for anyone passing by to see. He fired up the monitors and checked in with the teams. Everyone sounded as bored as he was.

"Make a note of the Manchester United match tonight and let me know how they do," Sean said, and that was about it.

Things can get boring, even when you're waiting for someone to try and kill you. Seconds seemed to take a minute, and the minutes dragged by like hours. He sent McCabe a text message that everything was ok. He checked the monitors four separate times over the course of the afternoon. He might as well have been looking at a black and white photograph for all the activity he saw.

He started a fire in the living room fireplace using the turf left in the bag, then fried up a steak and the last two potatoes for dinner. He headed back into the metropolis of Ballyboden to make his appearance for the evening a little after seven.

On the way back into town, he noticed a tire track out in front of the gate that had crossed his from earlier in the day. Maybe someone had just inadvertently veered onto the dirt and kept going. Maybe some locals had pulled over to see what the car was doing in front of the Connolly place. Or maybe someone was looking to make sure he was there. He thought about heading back to the house, getting on the monitors, and alerting the teams, but alert them to what? That some other car had gone down the lane? He couldn't even tell them when let alone what kind or how many may have been inside. He leaned back in the driver's seat and felt the pistol tucked into the small of his back, took a degree of comfort from it, and headed into Ballyboden.

Once in the village, he parked across the street from Bulger's pub, officially Bulger's Ballyboden House. It was a two-story white stucco building with black awnings stretched across the front of the place, and an entrance with double doors and stained glass. It was nice inside, almost too fancy for the likes of Dillon. There were actually two areas. One was a bar, sporting a granite bar top, glazed floor tiles, and nice stools. That area flowed into a larger room with gold sort of walls, a red pattern carpet, comfortable stools, and seating around tables. Large globes were attached to the walls for lighting. It wasn't more than half-past seven when he stepped inside, so only a handful of people were in the place.

No one turned a head as he approached the bar, and it dawned on him that this would be a watering hole for people taking hikes on various Dublin Mountain trails. A stranger like himself would be an everyday occurrence. The stools at the bar had a small back and a dark blue cushioned seat. He pulled one out, sat down, and waited for the barman to come and take his order. He was the only person seated at the bar.

He didn't have to wait long. "What can I get you?" the barman asked, then casually tossed a coaster down in front of Dillon. He pegged the barman to be in his mid-twenties with sharp blue eyes, and dark hair, already thinning on top and receding in front. His name tag read "Michael."

"Pint of Guinness," Dillon said.

Dillon watched as Michael poured the pint. It was a two-step process to do it properly and would take about three minutes. He picked up the sixteen-ounce Guinness glass, held it at a forty-five-degree angle, then opened the tap, pulling it toward him until the glass was filled halfway up the harp emblazoned on the side of the glass. He set the glass on the bar and let it sit as billions of nitrogen bubbles rose to the top. He was back about two minutes later, held the glass level, and pushed the tap back, filling the glass until the creamy head of foam rose just over the top of the glass.

"God, a work of art," Dillon said.

The barman smiled and asked, "American?"

"Yeah, Jack Dillon," he said, and extended his hand across the bar.

"Please to meet you," The barman said shaking his hand. "Umm, five-fifty for the pint."

Dillon threw a twenty-euro note on the bar, then sipped while he waited for his change. There was a thick brass plaque on the bar that read 'Est. 1798.' That meant over two hundred years of pouring, which suggested a lot of beer. He took his time and sipped.

There was a conversational hum in the place, but not loud enough to pick up what was actually being said. More people were coming in through the front door, but they all had the look of meeting up with friends, certainly not the crazy type of pub.

TWENTY-FIVE

She placed the flower, a single long-stemmed red rose, against the base of the large granite cross just like she'd done last week and the week before that. The cross was a ten-foot-high memorial immediately inside the entrance to the cemetery. It wasn't much, the effort, a simple act really, but under the circumstances, it was about all she could do. If she tried to claim her brother's body, it was a near certainty she'd be arrested and at best deported. At worst, she'd be arrested, jailed, and then deported after serving a sentence.

She made an orthodox sign of the cross, said a brief prayer for her brother, Borya, then hurried back out of the cemetery and down the street. She didn't notice the black vehicle parked across the street. But then why would she? She hadn't noticed when it followed her the mile and a half from her flat to the cemetery.

The large driver turned round in the front seat and glanced at the small man nervously fidgeting in the backseat. Without having to say anything, his expression asked the obvious question.

"I know, I know, I'm still thinking," the small man said. He sounded exasperated, indeed he was, nothing had worked thus far. Idiots. Amateur fools who'd seen too many movies. Now he was reduced to using a woman. A woman, for God's sake. As if the sneers and jeers, along with rumors of his inability to take control of matters, weren't bad enough. The malcontents below him whispered complaints to one another while the bosses above him, who would never think of getting their hands dirty, complained outright.

Still, if she was successful, he might be able to spin it as a clever move, using a woman. And if she failed, well, she was just a woman after all.

The driver continued to stare, awaiting instructions.

"All right, all right, yes, grab her. She'll be there to-night."

TWENTY-SIX

Dillon checked the clock on the wall and remembered McCabe wanted him back at the Connolly place no later than nine. He ordered a second pint and looked around some more. People were still drifting in, and the place was maybe half-full. He counted two couples, an older guy on his own and a blonde woman now seated at the bar.

His gaze caught the woman's eye, and she stared for a moment longer than normal, then looked away and sipped her drink, a glass of white wine. She wore a short-sleeve green dress with a scooped out neckline. The dress was maybe a little too fancy for a weeknight in a country pub, but it looked awfully nice. A large leather purse sat on the stool next to her. Maybe it was there to keep people away, or maybe she was saving the stool for someone else. He caught her looking at him again, actually studying him.

Michael, the barman, delivered his fresh pint, took the payment from the stash sitting on the bar, then walked to the far end of the bar and took an order from a couple who had just arrived. A woman pulled out a stool near Dillon and sat down. She glanced over at him, flashed a smile, then proceeded to study the various beer taps.

She was blonde, with hair that was parted in the middle, curled, and hung to her shoulders. She was pretty, in tight-fitting blue jeans, a white blouse, and a sweater with some sparkly effect to the yarn.

"What can I get you?" Michael asked.

"I think the Beck's if you please," she said. Her voice was slightly accented.

He delivered her beer and took her cash. She took a sip, set her glass back on the coaster, and looked over at Dillon. "It's too heavy for me, I'm afraid I don't like it," she said, indicating his glass of Guinness.

He figured a fifty/fifty shot, whether she just happened in or intentionally sat next to him.

"I'm sorry, my name is Eva," she said and extended her hand.

"Jack, Jack Dillon," he said, taking her hand and looking for some facial reaction when he told her his name. There wasn't one.

"You have an Irish name, but your accent, it is not Irish. You are maybe Canadian?"

He turned sideways on his stool, making it easier to gain quick access to his pistol. "No, American. And you? I'm not picking up an Irish accent."

She smiled. "German."

"Are you over on vacation? Working? Studying?"

"Sort of," she said and smiled. "The working, studying one. I'm on an internship, actually, online marketing."

"Your English is very good."

"Thank you, that's very kind. But I still have to,
umm, look up a lot of words that I hear or read. And then
there is the whole problem with the, how do you say it?
The slanger words?"

"Slang words."

"Yes, this is it."

"They have a lot of them over here. It's hard for me
to keep track of them all, and English is my native lan-
guage. Where are you from in Germany?"

"A small village in the south. I usually say Munich
when people ask because they have never heard of my
village."

"What's the name of it, your village?"

"Oh, well, my village, it's umm," she took a long sip
from her beer glass and seemed to take her time swal-
lowing before she responded. "Diessen. It's on the Ammersee. I'm sure you've never heard of it."

She seemed to hesitate, or was he just thinking that?
Was she buying time when she drank the beer, or was
she simply enjoying the beer?

"Actually, I have heard of it," he lied. "It's in Bavaria, right?"

She seemed to choke on her next sip, coughed a couple of times, then said, "Oh, you must excuse me."

To be honest, he'd never heard of the town, but if it was near Munich, then it was in Bavaria. She took out her cellphone, looked at him, and said, "Oh, sorry, would you excuse me for a moment." She placed the cell up against her ear, said something he figured was in German and hurried out of the bar. He didn't know if she was really talking to someone or just pretending.

He gazed down the bar, and the woman in the green dress raised her eyebrows very suggestively, then held his gaze.

He took a large swallow of Guinness, waited thirty seconds, then slipped off his stool and headed for the door. He stepped outside, looked around, but couldn't see the German woman on her cellphone.

He moved as quickly as he could without running and got in the car, pulled a U-turn in the middle of the street, and hurried back to the Connolly farm. He checked the rearview mirror every three or four seconds, but never saw anyone following. He turned onto the small lane and hurried toward the gate, then once he made the turn, he drove as fast as possible up to the house. He did a quick check around the front before he got out of the car and hustled inside.

Once inside, he turned on the monitors and checked in with the four teams. By now, he'd calmed down somewhat and decided it might be wise to keep the past fifteen or twenty minutes to himself. After he checked in, he used a computer to Google the German town of Diessen.

Sure enough there it was, on the Ammersee in upper Bavaria. He spent the next hour thinking about Eva, then climbed the stairs and went to sleep.

TWENTY-SEVEN

Dillon woke just a little after sunrise, exhausted and unrested with the blankets and sheet wrapped around him. He had an empty glass positioned in front of the bedroom door, thinking if someone entered, they'd knock it over and wake him. He'd slept on the floor in the farthest corner from the bed, and as an added precaution, had draped the bullet-proof vest over him. On the other hand, Lucifer was curled up on a pillow on the bed, sound asleep, and still snoring.

Dillon's back was stiff. His shoulder felt like he'd been carrying bricks all through the night. He had a throbbing headache and was mad at himself for leaving a half-pint of Guinness on the bar at Bulger's. He didn't want to even go near the thought of running away from the pretty German girl, Eva. After his stupid assumptions about her phone call, it had never dawned on him that she might be talking to a girlfriend, probably telling her she'd just met a really charming American. And the woman in the green dress, probably just the village working girl, or someone from Dublin working the vacation trade.

He groaned to his feet, then stumbled into the bathroom and took a long, hot shower. The shower somewhat revived him, and he wandered back into the bedroom.

Lucifer shot him a glance as Dillon got dressed, suggesting he could be a little quieter. He went downstairs, turned on the monitors, looked at all the security positions for the next half-hour, then made himself breakfast. He checked in with the teams around nine and pissed off Sean when he told him he forgot to check the Manchester United score. He drove back to Ballyboden at half-past eleven and purchased another steak from the butcher lady.

He grabbed a James Patterson novel off the rack next to the checkout lane in the grocery store. He made a point of thanking the cashier for pointing out the gas station the day before, but she didn't seem to recall the incident and looked at him like he was crazy.

He purchased another bottle of wine at O'Brien's bottle store and lied to the guy behind the counter, telling him he loved the hiking trail he'd recommended. That led to another fifteen-minute conversation that covered fauna and Paleolithic structures in the region. Dillon tossed the wine, the Patterson novel, and the steak in the car, then crossed the street to Bulger's Ballyboden House.

He took up residence on the same stool from which he'd fled the evening before. The barman, this one with the name tag "Kevin," raised his eyebrows at Dillon as he approached as if to say, "A bit early, isn't it?"

"I'll have a pint of Guinness," Dillon said before any words came out of the barman's mouth. He dutifully poured the pint, making the entire process appear even more grand than Michael, the barman from the night before. He presented the pint with a flourish, and Dillon handed him a ten-euro note. When he returned with the change, Dillon said, "Would you happen to know a German girl I ran into here last night?"

He smiled and said, "Which one?"

"She said her name was Eva."

"Not aware of one by that name."

"Blonde, thick curly hair, nice-looking. Said she was doing an apprenticeship over here in online marketing."

"Like I said, which one?"

"She was from some small village near Munich."

"Sorry, wish I could help you. Course, if I run into her, I might want to take a go at her myself. We have a lot of them coming through, what with the hiking trails and all. I hear they can be a handful." He followed that last bit with a smile, then wandered down the bar and started washing glasses.

Dillon lingered over the pint for longer than was prudent, then slid off his stool, gave a wave to the barman, called thanks, and headed out to the car. The bottle of wine, the steak lying next to it wrapped in a white plastic bag, and his new book sat on the passenger seat just where he'd left them. He climbed behind the wheel, made a U-turn, and headed back to the Connolly farm.

He checked the rearview mirror a handful of times, but all he saw was a middle-aged couple on bicycles. He pulled onto the small lane, then drove up to the gate, stopped the car, and got out. Remnants of the tire track that caught his attention yesterday could still be seen, along with a set of small footprints that appeared to head in through the gate then off into the brush on the side of the road. He climbed back in the car and drove up to the house, careful not to drive over the trail of footprints in case someone on the security team wanted to check them out.

He entered the house and called for Lucifer while standing at the front door. The dog peeked his head around the kitchen door and studied Dillon for a moment.

"Come on, let's go outside," Dillon said, and Lucifer hopped toward the open door. Once outside, the dog made a beeline for the rubble at the end of the house and sort of wiggled his way underneath the rusted metal roofing.

Dillon strolled over and gazed at the mess through what had once been a window. Rusted lengths of metal roofing, cracked pieces of weathered lumber, stones, weeds, and bits of glass. Over against the far wall, someone had smashed what looked like a whiskey bottle. If he'd had to guess, he'd say the thing had been thrown from about where he was standing.

He poked around for the better part of a half-hour, looked back from time to time at the small lane, and tried to figure out the best way to approach the house without being seen. He quickly decided maybe a half-mile down the lane in either direction and coming in through the fields along the side would make the most sense, but then that would run you right into one of the security teams.

The parking area along the front of the house was more or less dirt, with the occasional bit of weed popping up. He casually walked along it, looking for the odd foot-print, but found none. After twenty or thirty minutes, he called for Lucifer, and once he emerged, they headed back into the house.

He turned on the monitors, checked in with each se-curity unit, mentioned the set of small footprints to eve-ryone, but never received more than a grudging ac-knowledgment. No one had seen anyone. Nothing seemed out of the ordinary. After his earlier conversation with Kevin the barman, he was glad he hadn't mentioned the German girl, Eva, to the security units.

He wandered upstairs, retrieved the sheet and blan-kets from the corner of the bedroom, made the bed, ar-ranged the bulletproof vest on the edge of the bed, straightened the pillows Lucifer had slept on, then headed downstairs. He sent McCabe the 'All ok' text message, then made a cheese sandwich for lunch and opened up the Patterson book.

It was a sunny afternoon, and so he opened some windows in the living room and the kitchen, then went upstairs and did the same on the second floor. God only knew the place could certainly use an airing out. He lay down on the bed, continued reading the Patterson book, and the next thing he knew Lucifer was licking his face in an attempt to wake him. They went downstairs, then hustled out the door, the dog heading into his favorite pile of rubble as soon as they stepped outside.

Looking around, nothing seemed out of the ordinary. After maybe ten minutes, he gave a couple of whistles for Lucifer, and once he reappeared, they went back inside. Dillon fixed another steak for dinner, did a quick check on the monitors, then shut the system down and headed back to town to make his presence known.

TWENTY-EIGHT

I t was early enough in the evening that Dillon was able to grab the same parking place as the night before. He checked the mirrors for anyone on the street before he got out of the car. He didn't see anyone, so he climbed out, gave another look around, then headed into Bulger's.

It was just like the previous night, sparsely populated at this early hour. He grabbed the same barstool as last night and again earlier this afternoon. He caught Michael's eye at the opposite end of the bar, chatting with two redheaded women. He looked around but didn't see the German woman, Eva, anywhere. Michael gave him a nod as Dillon pulled out the stool. He finished telling his joke, waited while the redheads laughed, then walked down the length of the bar.

"Pint of Guinness?" he asked.

Dillon nodded, then gave a casual look around the room. He was thinking no one looked familiar when suddenly the blonde from the night before, the one in the green dress, came in the door. Tonight she was dressed in a short, tight red dress. She stared for a brief moment, maybe raised her eyebrows and licked her upper lip, he couldn't be sure, but she had definitely stared. She headed to the end of the bar, on the far side of the redheads, and pulled out a stool. Then she shot a definite look in Dillon's direction and held it for an overly long moment before she sat down.

Michael delivered his pint a moment later. "You going to stay and finish this one?" he laughed.

"Yeah, sorry about that. Got a phone call and had to run."

"Leaving a pint behind, she must have been special."

"She is," Dillon lied. "Hey, I was chatting with a girl here last night. German girl, thick curly hair, blonde, nice-looking. Wonder if you know her?"

"Lot's of Germans coming through here, a lot of them blonde. She have a name?"

"I think she said it was Eva."

He seemed to think for a moment, then shook his head. "No, sorry, not ringing a bell."

Dillon sat for the next twenty minutes nursing the pint and watching the room gradually fill up. It wasn't barroom crazy. More like people quietly talking over a drink and having a laugh.

He thought another woman sort of nodded at him, then realized it was Mike the barman she was looking at. She was with a guy Dillon guessed to be her husband. There was another table of what looked and sounded like college kids. At least two separate tables had people wearing hiking gear and carrying backpacks. Both tables had maps spread out in front of them, and they seemed to be tracking a route and discussing. He guessed either reviewing where they'd been that day or planning tomorrow's excursion.

He caught the blonde at the far end of the bar getting off her stool, slinging her purse over her shoulder and heading his way. He felt his pulse suddenly pounding in his head, and he touched the back of his jacket, felt the pistol tucked into his belt, although just now, it didn't seem to impart much comfort.

A soft voice behind him said, "So, back to finish your beer."

She looked to be in the same tight-fitting jeans from the night before and a silky, light-blue blouse. A small gold crucifix, on a very fine gold chain, hung around her neck. He glanced down the bar. The woman in the red dress was just pulling out the stool she'd left only a moment ago, sitting back down with a disgusted look on her face and signaling the barman.

He turned and smiled. "Eva. Hi. I was hoping I'd run into you here tonight."

"Oh, really, that's so nice of you to say. Sorry about last night, I had to go outside because it was hard to hear that phone call in here, my sister calling from Munich. When I came back, you were gone, and you had left your beer. I didn't know if it was something I said or—"

"No, nothing like that. Actually, just like you, I got a phone call and had to run off. An elderly neighbor," he said in response to her look. "She really shouldn't be living alone. She was having a problem with an outside door not closing. Rather than wait until this morning, I figured I'd just run over and take care of it last night."

"Oh, that's really so nice."

"Well, if I didn't, she'd be up half the night worrying, and then I'd be up half the night worrying that she was worrying. So in the end, I'm not that nice, I really just did it for my own sanity."

She laughed at that, then said, "Mind if I join you?"

"What? No, of course not, I'd love it. Like I said, I was hoping I would see you tonight."

She pulled out the stool next to him, half-turned it to face him, and sat down. They were close enough that their knees were touching. She smiled and seemed to look into his eyes.

"What can I get you? Please, it's my treat. Another Beck's?"

"I think tonight I will celebrate, maybe a, what is it the American women drink? This Cosmo thing?"

"Cosmo?"

"Yes. Your Sex and the City woman, Carrie, she is always drinking this drink."

"A Cosmopolitan."

"This is it, yes. That's the one."

"Wow, I think that series finished up over ten years ago."

"Really? Well, maybe in the States, but it's still running here. I try and watch it every Tuesday night, and if I can't, I tape it."

"Let's see if our barman knows the recipe for a Cosmopolitan." Dillon waved to get Mike's attention back, laughing it up with the redheads at the end of the bar. Once Mike nodded, Dillon glanced past the redheads. The blonde in the red dress stared back and ran her tongue slowly back and forth over her upper lip. Dillon felt his pulse beginning to pound again, not from lust, but rather fear.

"Yeah, Jack," the barman said a moment later and tossed a cardboard coaster advertising Smithwick's Blonde down in front of Eva.

"Mike, you know how to mix a Cosmopolitan for my friend here?"

"You mean with vodka, Cointreau, fresh lime juice, and cranberry juice?"

Eva giggled, and Dillon said, "Yeah, that's it."

"No, never heard of it. Just the one, or is this for both of you?"

"One for the lady, and I'll have another Guinness."

"Coming right up," he said.

He delivered the drinks and three more rounds over the course of the evening while they talked about everything and nothing. Eva explained the intricacies of online advertising. Dillon lied and said he was an accountant, which pretty much put a halt to any further conversation regarding his career.

She was beyond charming, and by her third Cosmo, she was rubbing his thigh more than occasionally. When he ordered another for her, she shook her head from side to side, then leaned over and gave him a long kiss, all the while squeezing his thigh. "I really shouldn't. When I drink this much, I start to lose all control."

"Is that a bad thing?"

"No. Actually, it can be a lot of fun, indeed," she said, then flared her eyes, smiled, and gave him another kiss. When she pulled back, the fresh drink was waiting for her.

TWENTY-NINE

His drunken thought was he would just sneak her into the Connolly place and then sneak her back out before breakfast. Based on his four or five pints of Guinness and Eva's four Cosmopolitans, it seemed like a reasonably logical plan. He helped her into the front seat of the car, then had to help her buckle up. She grabbed his hand, placed it between her thighs, then flared her eyes.

"Mmm-mmm, thank you," she slurred. "I'm sorry, I've gotten so drunk, but vodka seems to do this to me. Always. You shouldn't have bought all those drinks for me. Now I have to come up with a way to repay you."

Dillon had some ideas. He pulled a quick U-turn in the street and sped out of the village. He glanced in the rearview mirror at one point and saw a pair of headlights, but they had disappeared when he next looked.

As they drove, Eva giggled at her own dirty jokes. Dillon was staring at the buttons she'd undone on her blouse, and had to stop and back up fifteen feet after almost missing the turn onto the lane. Fortunately, Eva just mumbled something in German and giggled some more. In his haste, he scraped the car against the gate while turning into the Connolly place. There was a loud noise, and the side mirror on the driver's side was suddenly turned in. He raced up to the house and parked, then ran around to the passenger side and helped Eva climb out.

"Mmm-mmm, this is where you live, Jack? It's so, so out in the middle of nowhere," she giggled, and sort of steadied herself by leaning against the car. She pulled him toward her, gave him a long, passionate kiss, working her tongue in ways he'd forgotten were possible. She wrapped a leg tightly around him and forced him even closer.

He eventually extricated himself, took her arm, and guided her, giggling, toward the front door. He couldn't seem to get the keys out fast enough to unlock the door. When he opened it, Lucifer was right there and ran out the door, squeezed between the two of them, and headed for the rubble alongside the house. Eva watched him over her shoulder as Dillon guided her inside, and the door closed behind them.

"Would you like something to drink?"

"I think that's a great idea," she said, then sort of staggered a step or two and dropped her purse on the floor.

"How does a glass of red wine sound?"

"Perfectly delicious. Point me to your bathroom if you would, please."

"Just up at the top of the stairs and take a right."

She took three steps toward the staircase and one step backward. "I may need some help," she said, then grabbed onto the railing and began to pull herself up the stairs. The stair rail wiggled back and forth, and she half-stumbled. "Push me," she said over her shoulder.

Dillon picked up her purse, placed both hands on her perfect rear, and helped guide her up the staircase. "Mmm-mmm, wonderful," she said as he maneuvered her into the bathroom and turned on the lights. She entered the bathroom, turned to face him as she unbuckled her belt. "You can stay if you want."

"I'll just put your purse in the bedroom and get your wine," he said and closed the bathroom door behind him before she could respond. He made a quick calculation estimating how long it might take to fill the tub with the whirlpool jets as he carried her purse into the bedroom. He tossed the purse on the bed and then thought for half a second, glanced at the bathroom door, opened the purse, and rummaged through it. Probably a good thing, because there, on the bottom, beneath the billfold, the hairbrush, half a dozen makeup tubes, and a partially eaten candy bar, sat a small pistol.

It was very small, two short grey barrels, one on top of the other, no more than two and a half inches long. A derringer, actually. Printed along the barrels was 'Bond Arms Granbury Texas 45ACP.' Small black handgrips featured a five-pointed star. He pushed a silver button, cracked open the barrels, and removed two brass shells. Hollow points. Designed to leave an awfully large hole. He put the shells in his pocket, heard the toilet flush, quickly put the derringer back in her purse, and left the purse on the bed. He hurried down the steps toward the front door just as the bathroom door opened.

"Jack," she said, stepping out of the bathroom. "I have a better idea than wine. Much more fun. What do you think?" He turned to look at her now, standing at the top of the stairs in just a powder blue thong and bra, holding her jeans and blouse. "Interested?"

"Yes, very much." He started to turn and head back up the stairs when he heard scratching at the front door. "Oh, God, hold that thought," he said, then hurried down the stairs and pulled the door open to let Lucifer in. The dog ran inside, then stopped, looked up, and stared at Eva, still standing at the top of the stairs.

"Oh, so cute, what's the name?"

"Umm, Lou."

"Mmm-mmm, come here, Lou. Come here." Lucifer ignored her.

Dillon slowly climbed up the stairs, staring at her delicious figure and convincing himself she was unarmed. Eva kissed him as he reached the top, a long passionate kiss. Then she stepped back and handed Dillon her jeans and blouse. "I'll be there in just a moment. I just love little dogs." She suddenly didn't sound all that intoxicated. "Maybe you could get ready," she said with a raise of her eyebrow and pulled at his belt.

He nodded, hurried into the bedroom, pulled the pistol from the small of his back, and stuck it beneath the mattress. He grabbed the bulletproof vest, tossed it in a corner of the room, and covered it with his jacket. Just as he turned around, Eva strutted into the bedroom.

"Jack, I'm disappointed. You're still dressed? That won't be fun. Come here, and let me see what I'm going to get," she said, sitting down on the bed next to her purse. Dillon stepped in front of her, and she slowly unbuckled his belt. "I'm going to enjoy this," she said as she unbuttoned his jeans. She slowly pulled the zipper down, then looked up at him and licked her lips. "Mmmmmm, I've wanted this all night." She tugged on the jeans, pulled them down while still looking up at him, smiled, and said, "I think it's time we got started."

She had worked the jeans down around his knees and she suddenly rolled onto her back, pulling her legs back until her knees were almost touching her shoulders. "Ready?"

"This'll work," Dillon said, just as the smile left her face, and in one swift move, she placed a lightning rod kick into his ribs with both feet.

The blow knocked the wind out of him as he staggered back a step or two before tumbling backward onto the floor. She was off the bed in a second, kicked out in a karate stance, catching him on the side of the head with her heel as he struggled to his knees. He saw stars, and rolled off to the side, attempting to pull his jeans up. She spun to the opposite side in less than a second, leaned back on one leg, and thrust another kick that just narrowly missed his nose. She leaped forward and kicked with her opposite foot, catching him on the still-recovering shoulder and sending him sprawling across the wooden floor.

Lucifer hopped up onto the bed next to her purse and started barking as Dillon rolled a couple of times, attempting to get away from her, struggling to get back on his feet. She paused for a moment, quickly glanced from Dillon to her purse, and then back again.

He pretended to jump toward her purse. She kicked out at nothing, and he was able to sweep a foot behind her leg and knock her to the floor. Her head bounced off the wooden floor with an audible thump, but then just as quickly, she did a backward somersault and was on her feet. She kicked, spun and kicked again, moving Dillon toward the back of the room.

Lucifer continued barking.

Eva made some sort of half-step, kicked, missed, then caught Dillon in the ribs with a reverse kick that really hurt. He groaned and dropped onto the floor.

"Not much of a workout, Jack," she said, dumping her purse onto the bed, and grabbing the derringer. She pointed the weapon at him before he could even sit up, sort of flicked it toward the bed and said, "Why don't you just sit down and get comfortable? I have to say. I really expected something a little better. Americans, you never seem to miss the opportunity to disappoint."

He sat down roughly where he thought he'd stuffed the pistol.

"I feel like I've waited forever for this, Jack. Do you know anything about the men you murdered at the airport? Do you even know their names? Even care?"

"I know they were stupid. I know they failed, and I know—"

It seemed to take a long time, but in reality, it was just a second, maybe two at the most. Her eyes widened, then she screamed, "My brother, Borya, Borya Fedorov. This is for him." She thrust the derringer toward Dillon's forehead and pulled the trigger. *Click.* She looked wide-eyed at the tiny weapon in her hand, then thrust it toward him once more and pulled the trigger. *Click.*

He reached down between his legs and felt for the pistol beneath the mattress, moved his hand to the right an inch or two, and touched it just as Eva screamed, kicked him on the side of his forehead, and he saw stars. He fell sideways and bounced off the wall. She took a step toward him just as Lucifer sailed off the bed with his teeth bared and clamped onto her upper thigh. She screamed, spun around, hitting Lucifer over the head until he released and flew halfway across the room. She turned toward Dillon just as he shoved a hand beneath the mattress and grabbed the pistol. She spun him around with a vicious kick to the side of the head, half-jumped toward him to kick again as he raised the pistol, fired, and she went down.

Lucifer was up, shaking his head, growling, but not coming any closer to Eva writhing on the floor. It looked like he'd shot her in the knee. She rolled from side to side, clutching her knee with both hands and groaning as blood seeped through her fingers.

Dillon was still dizzy and slowly got to his feet by sliding his back up against the bedroom wall for support in an attempt to stand.

"Ahh, ahh, you bastard! Do something! Help me! My leg, oh God, my leg!"

He stepped over her, spread the pile of items dumped from her purse with his hand, making sure there wasn't anything that might be used as a weapon. There was nothing, really, unless she planned to spank him with the hairbrush. Downstairs, the front door suddenly banged open, and a voice he presumed was Sean Flynn shouted, "Dildo?"

Eva groaned, stopped rolling from side to side, and focused on him with a shocked look on her face.

"Yeah, Dildo," he said to her. "Too bad, you would have enjoyed yourself." Then he shouted, "Up here, Sean. It's all clear. Better call an ambulance."

THIRTY

Sean didn't call an ambulance. He did contact McCabe, who was now racing their way. One of the security team guys was a medic, to some extent. He gave Eva a shot of something that seemed to calm her down and ease her pain. Then he bandaged her knee as best he could.

Sean brought Dillon downstairs while another one of the guys did his best to clean up the blood on the bedroom floor. "Check the perimeter, bring the other teams in," he said to the two guys standing by the door. Once they left, he half-shoved Dillon into the kitchen and motioned toward a chair.

"Jack, sit the feck down. Can you see anything with your head that far up your ass? What the hell are you doing sneaking a woman in here? This isn't the States, you're—"

"She was going to kill me?"

"—liable to be charged with attempted rape. Not to mention, wait, what?"

"She's who they sent, the Russian gang. I met her last night at Bulger's in Ballyboden. She played drunk tonight, came on to me. She had a little pistol in her purse, a derringer sort of thing. I pulled these out of it earlier," he said, and dug the hollow points out of his pocket and placed them on the table in front of him. For the first time, he became aware of the almost three-day growth of beard along with the dirt and mud covering Sean's camouflaged clothes.

Sean picked up one of the hollow points, examined it, then looked at Dillon and smiled. "She do that to you?" he asked, and sort of indicated Dillon's face with his chin.

"She had no problem kicking the shit out of me, ka-rate kicks or some damn thing. She was pretty good," Dillon said, and suddenly his cheekbone, chin, shoulder, and ribs all seemed to begin throbbing at once.

"Once Peter's done bandaging her up, I'll have him take a look at you, make sure nothing's broken."

"Just my heart," Dillon joked.

"I'd say you're awfully damned lucky. You knew she was the one?"

Of course, he didn't, but he wasn't about to tell Sean that. He went on to tell him about Eva jumping on the phone the night before when she learned his name and told him about high tailing it back here to the Connolly place when he couldn't see her anywhere. "I figured she put the call into someone, told them where to find me. Then, when I saw her again tonight, and she pretended to be really shit-faced on just a couple of drinks, I figured I'd get her back here, and let you guys know." He was embellishing now, covering himself. "She asked if I knew anything about the three guys who were killed at the airport. I told her they were cowards, and that seemed to push her over the edge. She went nuts at that point. Apparently, one of them was her brother, Borya Fedorov, the only one that had been identified."

"Sean, hey, Sean," a voice called from upstairs.

Sean half-turned in his chair. "Yeah, Peter."

"Done about as much as I can up here. She's going to need a hospital."

"Shit," Sean said. "Can it wait a bit? McCabe's on his way out here. He could transport her back into Dublin. Keep her locked up once they finish their work."

"It can wait a bit, as long as he's on his way, but she's going to need attention."

"Come on down here and look at the dildo, she cleaned the floor with him."

"I don't want to leave her up here unattended."

"Good point. We'll come up." Sean looked at Dillon. "You okay with that?"

"Not a problem. I'd like to wish her good luck."

Eva, if that was even her real name, was lying on the floor, still in the thong and bra with a pillow beneath her head. She was just a few feet over from the bloodstained area on the floor where she'd been shot. Her knee was wrapped in a thick gauze bandage with a fresh blood stain about two inches in diameter. Her eyes looked glassy, and she seemed somewhat composed. She stared at Dillon when he stepped into the room.

The contents of her purse remained scattered across the end of the bed. Dillon looked around, didn't see her derringer anywhere, then spotted it under the bed. He grabbed her hairbrush and used it to slide the derringer out from beneath the bed.

"You got something we can wrap this up in, preserve her fingerprints?" he asked Sean.

"There might be a plastic bag downstairs. Did you see any in the kitchen?"

"No, but I know there's a paper grocery bag down there. I'll get it," Dillon said.

"That would be better than nothing."

He went down to the kitchen, pulled a paper bag out from between the refrigerator and the wall, and brought it back upstairs. Sean pulled a pen out of the pile of items dumped from Eva's purse, inserted the pen up the barrel of her derringer, and placed it in the paper bag.

"What are you going to do to me?" Eva asked. Her voice sounded thick and heavy.

"We'll get you to a hospital," Peter said, closing his medic kit.

"Then we'll lock you in a dark hole and just leave you there for a number of years," Sean added.

"You can't do that," she said, not sounding all that sure.

"Actually, we can and will. Well, unless there's something you could offer that might change our mind."

"I, I could pay you, all of you. Jack—" She sounded desperate.

"You'll have to do better than that, Eva. We don't need the money," Peter said, then looked away and rolled his eyes.

In the end, McCabe arrived along with O'Malley, two Garda cars, a van, an ambulance, and two guys from the local force. They were treating the Connolly place as a crime scene, sort of. The security teams were lined up and showering in the bathroom once they'd finished their glass of wine down in the kitchen. McCabe left, escorting the ambulance carrying Eva with flashing lights all the way to the hospital.

Sean Flynn and Dillon were the last two to leave the Connolly place. It was close to sunrise, and Lucifer was asleep in the backseat. As Sean pulled out of the small lane and onto the road, it suddenly dawned on Dillon that he was homeless.

"We don't have anywhere to go."

"What?"

"Lucifer and me." He yawned. "McCabe pulled us out of the hotel we were staying in. We don't have any place to go. We're essentially homeless, I think."

"I suppose I could drop you at the office and—"

"The office?"

"Yeah, I see what you mean. What about the apartment?"

"Where that guy shot up the bed in the middle of the night? Not very secure based on that, and it doesn't make any difference. I don't have keys."

Sean got a disgusted look on his face and glanced over at Dillon. "I suppose you could crash at my place. Just this once. But don't even think of unpacking your suitcase."

Dillon yawned again. "You got a washing machine? I'm on about the fourth time through wearing the same clothes. I go much longer they're going to get up and walk away under their own power."

Sean studied Dillon for a long moment, then refocused on the road. "Okay. You can do a load of laundry, but the first order of business, as soon as we go into the office, we find a place for you to land. You being at my place is going to cramp both our styles." But he smiled when he said it as they headed toward Ballyboden and back to Dublin.

EPILOGUE

At that hour of the early morning, Sean hurried through Ballyboden. He passed a blonde woman in a short, tight-fitting red dress. She had a purse slung over her shoulder and carried a wine glass. As Sean drove past, she raised her glass in a toast then staggered toward the front door of a cottage.

If only Dildo wasn't in the car, he thought. He glanced over at Dillon, already scrunched down and sound asleep in the passenger seat. So much for company, he was looking forward to catching a couple hours of sleep in his own bed tonight with the added luxury of sheets and blankets. Dillon could grab the couch in the sitting room. He sped past a black Mercedes parked in front of the small park without even noticing it.

The large man sitting behind the wheel watched the headlights approaching in his sideview mirror, then glanced over just in time to see the taillights continue down the road. He watched until they faded from view, then turned round to face the small man in the back.

Alexei Bazanov sat quietly, fidgeting in the backseat and staring blankly out the window. After a long moment, the driver said, "What do you want me to do?"

"Do? Christ forbid, nothing to do, but wait, and hope she turns up. Maybe the walk back was longer than she thought."

"She was supposed to be here hours ago. Told us she'd be here by midnight. The sun's about to rise. We—"

"I know, I know, damn it. You think I can't see what's happening?" he said then realized he was referring to a lot more than just the sunrise.

The End

Thank you for taking the time to read <u>Sweet Dreams</u>. If you enjoyed the read please take a moment and leave a review. Even if it's just a sentence or two the review really, really helps. Thank you . . .

Don't miss the sample of the next Jack Dillon Dublin Tale, <u>Mirror Mirror</u> on the following page.

ONE

It had been a little over two months since Dillon first arrived in Dublin, and things finally seemed to be settling down. He'd been living in the same unit for almost six weeks, and no one had tried to kill him. Lucifer, the black mutt he'd found tied to his door with an anonymous note describing him as impossible, was still with Dillon. He continued to work with the Irish cops, the Garda Síochána, and they hadn't threatened to deport him, at least lately. Abbey, his former neighbor with the long-stemmed roses tattooed on her lower back, had run into him on the street a few weeks back and was becoming an occasional friend with benefits.

He had his own vehicle, okay, it was a 2007 Opel Corsa, with almost a hundred and eighty thousand miles on it, the steering wheel on the right side and a stick shift he had to grind with his left hand, but still, he was getting used to it and hadn't side-swiped anything in a good two weeks.

He'd begun to take in some cultural things as well, learned a little more about the city, if not the island. He'd been to Trinity College, seen the Book of Kells, the vast library with over two hundred thousand books. He toured the GPO, the General Post Office, and Croke Park. He'd walked through Stephen's Green and spent an afternoon at the Guinness Brewery.

All well and good, but tonight was going to be special. Rather than spend another night in the pub, he had a guest coming over this afternoon, and he planned to wine and dine and, well…

* * *

"You sure you can't stay the night? You only just got here forty minutes ago. I was thinking I could cook you dinner or we could go up to the shops. There's a little place that does a great sushi." Dillon had taken both pillows, propped them up behind his back, and was in the process of watching Lin get dressed. At the moment, she was on her hands and knees looking for her thong.

"What'd you do with it? I mean, you just tossed it onto the floor, didn't you?" She looked up at Dillon as he took a sip of wine from her glass. "Hey, that's mine."

"Were you going to drink it?"

"Well, no, I'd like to, but I have to drive. We're just a little tougher with our laws over here than you are in the States."

"So, then, it's really not a problem if I take a sip."

She shot him a look.

"Okay, okay, sorry."

"You know, you could get out of bed and help me find the fecking thing. God, I just don't…."

"I would, but I'm just a little exhausted at the moment. I might be experiencing some sort of relapse and…."

"You're not experiencing any kind of relapse. You might be experiencing my foot up your hole if you don't help me. Besides, I checked your pulse, it was doing just fine if I recall."

"When did you check…oh, yeah," he said, remembering.

"So? Are you going to get your arse out of bed and help me?" she asked, then sat back on her heels with a puzzled look on her face.

He climbed out of bed with the notion that he knew exactly where her thong was.

"Now where do you think you're going?" she said as he walked out of the room.

He walked down the hall toward the bathroom. Lucifer, his ill-trained dog, was curled up against the spare room door, chewing something purple. Dillon reached down, grabbed the item, and quietly said, "Bad dog, but I get it." Lucifer looked up at him, then followed him back toward the bedroom, but had enough sense to head downstairs.

"Here, sorry, I guess Lucifer has a thing for you, too," he said and handed her what remained of her thong.

She held what was left of the item in both hands, then pulled the waistband and stared. "I can't wear this. There's literally nothing to wear."

"You want a pair of boxers?"

She rolled her eyes, picked the bottoms of her hospital scrubs up from the floor, and stepped into them. She slipped into her bra, hooked it from behind, then pulled the scrub top over her head. "God, you and your dog. He's just as bad as you."

"Sure I can't cook you some dinner, and then you could stay for breakfast?"

"I'd love to," she said, not sounding at all convincing. "But it's my three-day weekend. I've got a 10K run first thing in the morning for breast cancer and then tickets to the Leinster Munster match tomorrow night. I need to rest up." She stood on her tiptoes, gave him what barely passed as a peck on the cheek, then headed down the stairs.

"Bad dog," she said to Lucifer down on the first floor. "See you, thanks," she called, then closed the front door behind her and was gone.

Dillon watched her out the window as she climbed into her car. She sat behind the wheel, dialed her cellphone, and seemed to launch into an animated conversation as she pulled away.

He had two steaks marinating downstairs in the kitchen, an unopened bottle of wine on the counter he'd purchased especially for the night, and new candles in Waterford holders. So much for a relaxing evening at home.

TWO

Weston Airport is a small, private airport located just outside of Dublin, in County Kildare. It sits in a tranquil, rural setting and consists of one small runway just large enough to handle smaller, private planes. It features a restaurant, a bar, and a decently sized hangar with a number of small, private planes parked on the grass outside. The airport closes down at 8:30 in the evening during the summer months.

It was a good half-hour before closing when a small plane made its final approach. The plane glided along the runway for a bit, touched ground, skipped slightly just once, then cruised toward the end of the runway where it turned and headed toward the large hangar. As it neared the hangar a heavy, dark blue, Mercedes van drove around the corner of the building and slowly pulled in front of the hangar.

The vehicle was a cash-in-transit van designed to do exactly what the name suggested, move cash. It was square-built with heavy steel walls and solid tires, what would be called an armored van in the States. Small, bulletproof windows were imbedded in the rear of the van. A warning was posted on the rear door alerting everyone to the fact that the cash contents were attached to dye packs in the event of a robbery.

Two armed, uniformed men sat and waited in the van. Neither one spoke, but then what was there to say? They'd both done this dozens of times. They watched as the small plane approached. It moved up to the hangar, then turned, pulled forward maybe twenty feet, and a moment later shut down.

The cash-in-transit van pulled alongside the plane, and the uniformed individual in the passenger seat stepped out of the van. He was armed with an automatic weapon and wore a protective vest beneath his uniform.

The small side door on the plane opened, and someone handed what looked like a grey case out the door to him. He hurried to the rear of the van, opened the door, and set the case inside. A slightly built gentleman climbed out of the plane carrying an identical case, followed him to the rear of the van, and handed the case to the uniformed man. He set the case inside the van, closed the doors, and gave a final, cautious look around the area.

The slightly built man smiled, nodded, waved farewell, and then hurried back to the small airplane. As soon as he closed the door, the plane turned around, taxied to the end of the runway, and a moment later was cleared for takeoff.

The men in the van watched through the windshield as the plane traveled down the runway, picked up speed, hopped twice before it launched in the air, and sixty seconds later disappeared into the clouds.

They waited a moment, then made a gradual U-turn and headed back across the mostly empty parking lot. They stopped at the far end of the parking lot for a vehicle with its bright lights on to pass so they could turn.

The driver of a vehicle in the back of the parking lot said, "All right, perfect, I can see you coming down the road."

"I don't know, do you think they'll even stop?" The woman approaching the parking lot asked.

"They already have. You're doing just fine, just fine," he said, working to keep his voice calm. She'd no business being involved, and yet here she was, which meant he had to keep her on the straight and narrow. Just a minute or two more, and it would all be over, then good riddance to both her and the boyfriend.

THREE

He'd developed a taste for the stuff, Guinness. Based on its history, Dillon viewed it more as a health drink than a beer. Up until recently, it was offered as a daily ration to patients in hospital, so there were bound to be health benefits to a pint, which led him to his current off-duty undertaking. Just now, he was in the process of appraising another cultural icon of Ireland, the pub.

He was in the Palace Bar, the back room of the Palace, actually, seated with his back to the wall in an armed chair. He'd been thinking about Lin and her rather hasty departure this afternoon when he noticed the three women looking for a place to sit in the crowded room.

They were blondes, with thick hair, and from their appearance, he guessed sisters. He had a small table in front of him, with three empty stools alongside the table.

The women glanced at the stools but didn't make a move toward them, which marked them as tourists. That and the fact that they all had shopping bags from Carroll's, the Irish souvenir shops that were scattered on just about every other corner throughout Dublin city center.

It was Thursday night, and the room was jammed. Another crowd was drinking outside on the sidewalk, with more people coming in the door every minute. For the moment, it looked like Dillon controlled the only three available seats in the place.

"You want to sit down?" he called and sort of gestured toward the available stools.

They looked at each other for a long moment, a look on each face suggesting there had to be something better, somewhere. Two Dub's stepped into the room, scanned the place, spotted the open stools, and took a step toward them.

One of the women, she looked to be the oldest of the three, tossed her shopping bag a good ten feet. The bag landed on top of a stool perfectly, slid across it, and up against the table.

"Where were you guys?" Dillon said, hoping to make it sound like he'd been waiting for them. They smiled, hurried over, and sat down. The two Dubs frowned, turned, and retreated toward the crowded barroom.

"Is it okay if we sit here?" the woman who so expertly tossed the shopping bag asked as she sat down. She had an American accent.

"Not a problem. Everyone does it. I mean they at tables with folks they don't know. You're from the States?"

"Wisconsin," they all chimed in.

It fit. Blonde hair, blue eyes, beautiful skin. "Whereabouts in Wisconsin?"

"Milwaukee. Ever hear of it?" one of them asked, then proceeded to not wait for an answer. "We're just a little north of Chicago. On Lake Michigan. It's one of our Great Lakes, Michigan is. Well, and it's a state too, of course not the one we live in." She wore black jeans, black Nike shoes, and a sort of creamy-colored sweater. Her hair was pulled back in a bun, and she sat up very straight, ramrod straight. Dillon pegged her in the late thirties, maybe forty, but no more than that, and probably a school teacher.

"Isn't it great? You invite us to sit down, and we give you a geography lesson for free." This from the woman next to the teacher. She half shrugged and wrinkled her nose when she talked. She looked the youngest of the three. She would have been the spacey one.

"Carol," said the teacher. "He probably has never heard of Milwaukee, doesn't know about the Great Lakes and…"

"And is now regretting that he made the offer for us to sit down in the first place. Thanks." The oldest of the three smiled and extended her hand. "I'm Chris. This is my sister Carol and my sister Cindy."

Dillon shook her hand, said, "Nice to meet you. I'm Jack."

Chris held his hand for a moment. Carol shrugged and wrinkled her nose. Cindy, the school teacher, flashed a cold smile and pulled her jacket a little tighter around her shoulders.

"How long are you here for?" he asked.

"Four days, then back to the States. Sort of a whirl-wind tour. We saw all of Dublin today. Blarney Castle and then over to the Cliffs of Moher tomorrow. Westport, in County Mayo, where our family is from the next day."

"We're Irish." Carol shrugged and wrinkled her nose again.

"Oh, I thought you were American."

All three of them looked surprised at the response.

"Americans always say they're Irish, but the truth is they're American. They don't speak Irish, aren't from this country, wouldn't know what the GAA is or who's the Taoiseach."

"Do all Irish people hold that sort of opinion of Americans?" the school teacher named Cindy asked, and pulled her jacket even tighter.

"I wouldn't know, I'm an American."

"American? From where?"

"I guess all over, but mostly the midwest. Most recently, the East coast."

"New York I bet, everyone's crabby there," Carol, the youngest, said.

"I'll get our drinks," the school teacher said.

"White," said Chris.

"Red," said Carol and wrinkled her nose again. Dillon was beginning to think it might be some sort of an involuntary twitch. "Where's the ladies' room?" Carol asked. He pointed to a set of stairs leading down to a lower level. "Back in a minute," she said and hurried away, unbuckling her belt at the top of the stairs. Cindy was right behind her.

"Oh, God, give me strength." Chris, the only one left at the table, gave an exasperated sigh.

"Long day?" Dillon asked.

"Yes. I mean, no, they're really great, it's just that we're sisters. You know, plenty of lady drama. Someone doesn't like the food, or the noise or the fact that that there's no ice cubes in the glass of water. They remember something one of us said at Thanksgiving dinner three years ago. Or, they remember some perceived slight from high school. Whatever. Like I said, sisters."

"Nice you could all travel together."

"Yeah, at the end of the day, we're very lucky, and we know it."

They chatted for a couple of minutes. Dillon caught Carol and Cindy out of the corner of his eye, coming back up the steps from the ladies' room a few minutes later. They headed for the bar. Their older sister shook her head. "I know Cindy. She's going to ask to see the wine list, and then she'll want to argue with the bartender about which wine tastes like plums or cherries."

"They're four deep at the bar, waving twenty-euro notes to get a pint. This might not be the best place or the best time. Besides, I don't think they have a wine list. Probably just the same five or six they'll recite off the top of their head. Pints and whiskeys are more the thing here."

"She'll try anyway," she said, shaking her head.

The sisters were back ten minutes later. Cindy set a glass of white wine down in front of her sister. "Lots of luck, God knows what it tastes like. They don't even have a wine list."

"Jack was just telling me it's more of a pint and whiskey place."

"They could do a lot of business if they had a decent wine list," Cindy said, took a sip from her glass, and winced. "Oooh."

Dillon looked around the packed backroom. There wasn't an available stool in the place, and customers were standing and chatting in the few areas with enough room. The barroom was packed, literally four deep waving cash for a drink, and the four bartenders were filling pint glasses as fast as proper pouring allowed. A crowd of twenty or thirty stood out front on the sidewalk, drinking pints. The last thing the Palace needed was a fancy wine list.

He felt his phone vibrating in his pocket, pulled it out, and looked at the screen. McCabe. Shit.

FOUR

Now what, he thought. "Excuse me, I have to take this. Hello," he said, waited a moment, then said, "Hang on for just a moment, I'm moving to a quiet spot where I can hear you. Pardon me, ladies." Cindy, the school teacher, put a disgusted look on her face. He began to wedge his way through the crowd, heading for the front door. It took a couple of minutes, getting past a couple of over-served jerks who didn't think they should have to move, but he finally made it out the door and stepped onto the cobblestone street. "McCabe, you still there?"

"Where in the bleeding hell are you?"

"Out in front of the Palace. I couldn't hear you inside, and the place is packed, took a couple of minutes to get out. What's up?"

"We could maybe use your expertise."

"You debating which pub pours a better pint?"

McCabe ignored Dillon's attempt at humor. "Someone hit a cash-in-transit van. We've got two wounded. Apparently, the shooter was American or sounded American. I'm remembering your involvement with your man who robbed the armored car in New Jersey."

"Eddie Fleming? Yeah, but he's serving ten years in…"

"He's out."

"What do mean he's out? He was just…"

"Escaped, maybe six weeks ago. We apparently received an alert he was headed over here. One of our geniuses in the security office decided it would make more sense to sit on the information."

"Where are you now?"

"You're going to love it, Weston Airport."

"Not Dublin?"

"It's a small private airfield. Can you get to your car?"

"It's just a couple blocks away."

"Get onto the M4. Weston is in Leixlip, County Kildare. Take exit 5 on the M4, get onto the R403. See you in thirty minutes," he said and disconnected.

Dillon gave a longing look back toward the front door of the Palace. The three American women could argue about the wisdom of a wine list, who stole their boyfriends in high school, and why there wasn't any ice in the glass of water one of them would undoubtedly want. But they'd be doing it by themselves, without the grace and charm he always brought to the table. He took off at a trot toward his car.

He'd parked a good two blocks away, but knew he was lucky to even find a parking place he could squeeze into. Dublin wasn't exactly known for its parking options, and the few ramps they did have cost an arm and a leg if you were lucky enough to even find a space once you got into a ramp.

Mercifully his car wasn't clamped, and it hadn't been broken into. The Corsa sputtered to life on the second try, and he spent the next fifteen minutes getting out of the city center and making his way to the M4, a version of the interstate in the US, complete with bumper-to-bumper traffic jams during morning and afternoon rush hours.

To be continued . . .

Thanks for checking out <u>Mirror Mirror</u>. Things are about to get crazy for Marshal Jack Dillon. Better grab a copy to learn what happens . . .

Check out the list on the next page of books by Mike Faricy.

BOOKS BY MIKE FARICY
CRIME FICTION FIRSTS

A boxset of the first four books in four crime fiction series:

Russian Roulette; Dev Haskell series
Welcome; Jack Dillon Dublin Tales series
Corridor Man; Corridor Man series
Reduced Ransom! Hot Shot series

The following titles comprise the Dev Haskell series:

Russian Roulette: Case 1
Mr. Swirlee: Case 2
Bite Me: Case 3
Bombshell: Case 4
Tutti Frutti: Case 5
Last Shot: Case 6
Ting-A-Ling: Case 7
Crickett: Case 8
Bulldog: Case 9
Double Trouble: Case 10
Yellow Ribbon: Case 11
Dog Gone: Case 12
Scam Man: Case 13
Foiled: Case 14
What Happens in Vegas… Case 15
Art Hound: Case 16
The Office: Case 17

Star Struck: Case 18
International Incident: Case 19
Guest From Hell: Case 20
Art Attack: Case 21
Mystery Man: Case 22
Bow-Wow Rescue: Case 23
Cold Case: Case 24
Cash Up Front: Case 25
Dream House: Case 26
Alley Katz: Case 27
The Big Gamble: Case 28
Bad to the Bone: Case 29
Silencio!: Case 30
Surprise, Surprise: Case 31
Hit & Run: Case 32
Suspect Santa: Case 33
P.I. Apprentice: Case 34
Rebel Without a Clue: Case 35
Puppy Love: Case 36

The following titles are Dev Haskell novellas:
Dollhouse
The Dance
Pixie
Fore!
Twinkle Toes
(*a Dev Haskell short story*)

The following are Dev Haskell Boxsets:
Dev Haskell Boxset 1-3
Dev Haskell Boxset 4-6
Dev Haskell Boxset 7-9
Dev Haskell Boxset 10-12
Dev Haskell Boxset 13-15
Dev Haskell Boxset 16-18
Dev Haskell Boxset 19-21
Dev Haskell Boxset 22-24
Dev Haskell Boxset 25-27
Dev Haskell Boxset 28-30
Dev Haskell Boxset 1-7
Dev Haskell Boxset 8-14
Dev Haskell Boxset 15-19
Dev Haskell Boxset 20-24
Dev Haskell Boxset 25-29

The following titles comprise the Jack Dillon Dublin Tales series:
Welcome
Jack Dillon Dublin Tale 1
Sweet Dreams
Jack Dillon Dublin Tale 2
Mirror Mirror
Jack Dillon Dublin Tale 3
Silver Bullet
Jack Dillon Dublin Tale 4
Fair City Blues

Jack Dillon Dublin Tale 5
Spade Work
Jack Dillon Dublin Tale 6
Madeline Missing
Jack Dillon Dublin Tale 7
Mistaken Identity
Jack Dillon Dublin Tale 8
Picture Perfect
Jack Dillon Dublin Tale 9
Dublin Moon
Jack Dillon Dublin Tale 10
Mystery Woman
Jack Dillon Dublin Tale 11
Second Chance
Jack Dillon Dublin Tale 12
Payback Brother
Jack Dillon Dublin Tale 13
The Heist
Jack Dillon Dublin Tale 14
Jewels To Kill For
Jack Dillon Dublin Tale 15
Retirement Scheme
Jack Dillon Dublin Tale 16
The Collector
Jack Dillon Dublin Tale 17

Jack Dillon Dublin Tales Boxsets:
Jack Dillon Dublin Tales 1-3
Jack Dillon Dublin Tales 4-6

Jack Dillon Dublin Tales 1-5
Jack Dillon Dublin Tales 1-7
Jack Dillon Dublin Tales 6-10

The following titles comprise the Hotshot series;
Reduced Ransom! Second Edition
Finders Keepers! Second Edition
Bankers Hours Second Edition
Chow Down Second Edition
Moonlight Dance Academy Second Edition
Irish Dukes (Fight Card Series)
written under the pseudonym Jack Tunney

The following titles comprise the Corridor Man series:
Corridor Man
Corridor Man 2: Opportunity knocks
Corridor Man 3: The Dungeon
Corridor Man 4: Dead End
Corridor Man 5: Finger
Corridor Man 6: Exit Strategy
Corridor Man 7: Trunk Music
Corridor Man 8: Birthday Boy
Corridor Man 9: Boss Man
Corridor Man 10: Bye Bye Bobby

Corridor Man novellas:
Corridor Man: Valentine
Corridor Man: Auditor

Corridor Man: Howling
Corridor Man: Spa Day

The following are Corridor Man Boxsets:
Corridor Man Boxset 1-3
Corridor Man Boxset 1-5
Corridor Man Boxset 6-9

THANK YOU!

Contact the author:
- Email: mikefaricyauthor@gmail.com
- Twitter: @Mikefaricybooks
- Facebook: Mike Faricy Author
- Website: http://www.mikefaricybooks.com

Published by

MJF Publishing

9 781962 080637